DOCTOR WHO
AND THE ZARBI

DOCTOR WHO AND THE ZARBI

Based on the television serial *Doctor Who and The Web Planet* by Bill Strutton by arrangement with the British Broadcasting Company

BILL STRUTTON

Illustrated by John Wood

A TARGET BOOK
published by
the Paperback Division of
W. H. Allen & Co. Ltd

A Target Book
Published in 1973
by the Paperback Division of W. H. Allen & Co. Ltd
A Howard & Wyndham Company
44 Hill Street, London W1X 8LB

Reprinted 1978
Reprinted 1979
Reprinted 1981
Reprinted 1982

Novelisation copyright © 1965 by Bill Strutton
Original script coyright © 1965 by Bill Strutton
Illustrations copyright © 1965 by W. H. Allen & Co. Ltd
'Doctor Who' series copyright © 1963 by the
British Broadcasting Corporation

Printed in Great Britain by
The Anchor Press Ltd
Tiptree, Essex

ISBN 0 426 10129 4

Contents

CHAPTER ONE

The Web Planet

It was almost quiet inside *Tardis*. There was only a slight hum from the control column, where Doctor Who bent and peered at his instruments. He flipped a switch. A panel on the ship's control board glowed. A needle on it flickered into life, unsteadily at first. Then it began dancing wildly back and forth across the scale.

Doctor Who stared and frowned.
'Strange,' he muttered. 'Very strange . . .'
He flipped on the space scanner switch and stared up at the screen. A harsh, crackling sound invaded the ship and the screen was suddenly speckled with brilliant, dancing bursts of light.
The sound made Ian turn. He had finished dressing before

a mirror panel and was knotting his favourite tie – his Coal Hill Old Boys' tie – when he saw the screen. The blobs of light on it pulsed and grew, then exploded in dazzling bubble shapes. The crackling sound was growing louder.

Ian finished tying his tie and crossed to the control column. He stared up.

'What is it, Doctor?'

Doctor Who was too intent to answer for a moment. The bursts of light from the space scanner screen lit his face. He flicked on the power response switches. The needles on the lighted dials of his control panel, instead of rising steadily to give a reading, jerked crazily into life, and began flickering wildly all over the scale.

He said, 'Try the time calculator, Chesterton. Tell me what reading you get.'

Ian press the time button. The pointer on the time scale rose jerkily from zero. It climbed in a series of unsteady spurts and hovered for a moment. Ian stared closer.

'About 7000 B.C.' He paused. 'No – wait!'

The time pointer dropped, rose giddily on the scale, plunged again.

'It's gone haywire! We could be at any point in time between 7000 B.C. and about A.D. 200000! Look!'

Doctor Who turned to share Ian's inspection of the time calculator scale. His face was grave. He said nothing, but turned slowly back to fix his gaze on the cluster of instruments immediately in front of him on the big control panel.

Behind them the door of the dormitory section slid open and Barbara stepped into the control room. She stopped at the sight of the bursting lights on the scanner and at the harsh crackling.

'What's happening?'

There was a pause. Doctor Who turned to Barbara and hesitated. He smiled.

'Just a little, um, interference, my dear. Nothing ... unusual. Er, would you like to get us some coffee?'

But Barbara stood her ground. 'Something's wrong, isn't it?'

8

'Nothing for you to worry about,' Doctor Who said, in his most soothing voice. But his gaze was drawn back to his instruments. He was clearly puzzled, and he wagged his silvery head over them.

Ian grinned at Barbara. 'It's nice to see you up and dressed,' he said. 'Does that mean we can expect some bacon and eggs?'

Barbara looked towards the figure of Doctor Who frowning over his controls.

'I'll see what I can do.'

Then they all stiffened as the crackling sound from the scanner now began to rise weirdly in pitch, growing immensely loud, while the light bursts gathered and multiplied until the screen was as dazzling as a firework display.

Barbara stared in alarm at Ian.

'Won't somebody tell me what's happening?'

Ian switched off the time calculator and came swiftly to join Doctor Who. He took one look at the needles on the dials there, some flickering madly, others quivering near zero.

'Your instruments, Doctor! They've *all* gone mad! Why? What can be doing all *that* to them?'

Doctor Who was shaking his head grimly.

He muttered slowly. 'I don't know. I ... suppose we could have materialized for a split second of time, and been caught in the ... influence ...'

'Influence? What influence?'

Doctor Who raised his head and looked at both Ian and Barbara.

'We seem to have been imprisoned by some kind of ... force. I can't break the hold at all.' He paused. 'Something, somewhere, is slowly pulling us – plucking us down ...'

'Something ... pulling us down?' Barabara said. Her voice shook a little and some of her alarm showed in her eyes. 'Down to where?'

Doctor Who shrugged and gestured to his control panel.

How can I tell?' he snapped, 'when not one of my instruments will give us a sane reading?'

A pause. The crackling rose even higher, and Ian could

not look at the dazzling pattern of light on the scanner without shielding his eyes.

'So we don't know where we are – or at what point in time?'

Doctor Who waved his hand irritably for silence.

'Please! No time for questions! The important thing is to pull the ship clear of – this . . . whatever it is!' He pointed at the space scanner, and added in a mutter, 'If we can . . .'

Ian stared at Doctor Who, then at Barbara.

'*If* we can?'

Doctor Who flared impatiently. 'Chesterton, will you kindly stop gaping and give me a hand with the power boost! Before it's too . . .'

A cry from Barbara interrupted them. 'The scanner – look!'

Doctor Who and Ian paused in the act of reaching for the booster switches. They stared up. The dazzling blobs of light were fading from the scanner screen. It was slowly clearing. With it the harsh crackling sound was vanishing too.

'We're clear!' Ian shouted excitedly. 'It's gone!'

Doctor Who was peering intently at the screen. He cast a glance towards his instruments, checking them. He shook his head.

'No,' he said. 'We are *not* clear. In fact . . .'

Doctor Who paused, thinking, ignoring the others.

'In fact *what*?' Ian asked.

Doctor Who raised his head. 'The ship is out of control – our control anyway.' He said it almost absently.

'But the interference has gone! Look at the scanner! It's clear!'

Doctor Who turned his head to look at Ian. He snapped, 'Look at our *instruments*!'

Ian stared at the control dials.

'They're still all over the place! They don't make any sense!'

'Quite! And until we can get them to respond properly, we can do nothing!'

Out of the worried silence Barbara said, faltering, 'You mean – we are stuck?'

Doctor Who shrugged. He turned to Ian and said curtly, 'Switch on the searchlight, Chesterton.'

Ian obeyed, snapping on the searchlight toggle. They all peered at the local inspection window as the ship's searchlight began revolving, probing their immediate surroundings.

As they looked, their youngest companion in the ship *Tardis*, the girl Vicki, came sleepily out of the dormitory, fumbled at the sliding door, and entered the control section, yawning. She stopped at the sight of Ian, Barbara and Doctor Who, all staring at the inspection screen. Barbara turned.

'You should be in bed,' she said. 'You've had hardly any sleep.'

'Where are we?' Vicki asked.

The others looked at Doctor Who for an answer. After a moment he wagged his head and muttered, 'I wish I knew.'

'What are you all looking at the screen for? Is there ... something out there?' Vicki asked.

No one answered for a moment. Then the searchlight beam sweeping round in a circle from the ship, lit on a craggy shape. Doctor Who straightened, still staring at the screen.

'Yes,' he said. 'There is.'

The light on this planet was pale and cold, like moonlight, and peopled with harsh shadows. Strange, pointed crags like large stalagmites rose here and there from its surface. Several satellites glowed faintly in the twilit sky. Beyond them glimmered a few distant stars.

It was near one of the crags that the police-box shape of the ship *Tardis* slowly materialized, appearing as if from nowhere. Its searchlight beam circled, exploring the place, swept over a crag, hovered, and held it in its light.

The beam passed on, inspecting the planet slowly, and slowly flooded over a pool. A faint mist rose from the pool.

The searchlight continued to turn, lighting up a glassy surface scattered with small rocks, creating eerie moving fingers of shadow as the ray revolved.

It was as quiet and as ghostly as a cemetery. There was no sound, not even a wind.

Then a slithering, scraping noise broke the stillness. It came from a crag whose shape reared steeply out of the ground some fifty yards away, just beyond the wash of the searchlight, silhouetted blackly against the orb of a satellite.

Something high on this crag moved.

A long thin foreleg came into sight, gripping the rock. The moving leg shone in the faint light like gun-metal. Then a sleek, shiny head appeared, and with it, two eyes which shone like large torch bulbs. These eyes turned in the direction of the ship and fixed steadily on it.

Then the creature gave a harsh chirruping sound, like a cricket. It echoed and re-echoed in the uncanny stillness.

The sound was answered from another direction.

There, too, the eyes of another shone from the shadowy side of a crag.

The local inspection screen inside *Tardis* was now picking out the features of this strange landscape more clearly as the searchlight turned further.

'Do you recognize it?' Ian asked Doctor Who.

But Doctor Who seemed too busy checking his instruments and watching the inspection window to reply. He transferred his stare to the scanner as it started to speckle again with small spots of light.

'This interference!' he muttered. 'Most extraordinary – in a place like this . . .'

'There can't be anything out there, surely?' Ian said. 'It looks as dead as a dodo.'

'Really?' Doctor Who muttered.

'Just crags and pools,' Barbara said. 'No movement . . . nothing growing. Not a living thing in sight.'

A gasp came from Vicki. She clapped her hands to her ears. The others turned and stared at her.

'What's the matter?' Barbara asked.

'My ears! There *is* something! Listen!'

The others listened a moment, and looked blank.

'Can't *you* hear it?' Vicki cried. She screwed up her face, pressed harder on her ears. 'Oh! It's so ... piercing, it hurts!'

'It's probably your ears singing,' Ian said. 'Try swallowing.'

Doctor Who was looking keenly at Vicki.

'—or something extra-sonic,' he murmered. 'Something so high-pitched that only children or animals pick it up ... what kind of sound, my dear?

'A sort of ... humming, very high! You must be able to hear it! Please, make it stop! It's going right through me!'

'Shall I switch off our detectors? Ian asked.

Doctor Who nodded. But suddenly Vicki took her hands away from her ears. Her face cleared. The relief seemed so great that she smiled, puzzled.

'It's gone!' she said. 'It's stopped!'

Ian's hand was poised over the switches on the control table. He looked at the dials and called abruptly.

'Doctor! Some of our instruments are responding!'

He pointed. The time pointer was wavering unsteadily near the A.D. 20000 mark.

Doctor Who crossed to his side.

'So it is. Hmm. Now the question is, what's been causing these failures? What kind of ... force, eh? Look – dimension scale – negative response. Astral computer – out of order! Gyros at Zero. Now what *can* be holding us here?'

'Holding us?' Ian said. 'Couldn't it just be that something is wrong with *Tardis*?'

'Certainly not!' Doctor Who snapped. 'We did not stray into this place through any mechanical fault. We've been plucked off course by ... something. Now – is it some natural phenomenon ... or something intelligent ... deliberate? With ... a purpose?'

'You mean – something more powerful than the ship?' Vicki asked a little wide-eyed.

Doctor Who waved a reassuring hand.

'Whatever it is, I'm, er, sure I can find an answer to it. Chesterton, we'll try maximum power. Switch on boosters. Let's see if they'll lift us clear of . . . this place.'

Barbara stared at the forbidding landscape through the inspection screen and shivered. 'I hope so,' she murmured.

Ian snapped on all five booster switches. There was a steady hum of machinery in response, rising slowly in volume. Doctor Who's face cleared a little as he heard it and watched the power response dials.

'Power's responding,' Ian reported.

'Yes, yes. Wait till it reaches maximum before we switch on the motors.'

Behind them Vicki relaxed a little, her face clearing. She rubbed her temples.

'I can't wait for us to get away from here,' she said. 'I never want to hear that sound again. Not ever!'

The comforting hum of the ship's motors continued to rise steadily. Ian looked across at Doctor Who, but the old man never took his eyes off the power response dials. He grunted, 'Mm! Power build-up very satisfactory.'

He paused, waiting, watching the dials, his hand straying to hover over the motor levers.

'Now – motors!'

He snapped the levers down and scanned the instrument confidently.

'They're responding!'

The police-box shape of *Tardis*, nestling in a space between the crags, gave out a powerful whirring from its motors and its outlines began to fade until it was almost transparent against the strange lunar background of the planet.

But away on a neighbouring crag, movement showed again – and sound. There was a slithering. The eyes of the watching creature shone out of the shadows. Its feelers came into sight, manhandling something, and a slim cylinder appeared from behind a ledge of rock.

It was manoeuvred into position and could now be clearly

seen – a strange barrel, sleeved in a coil of something which looked like glass tubing, mounted on a conical base.

The slim, shiny forelegs of the creature swivelled this cylinder downward until it pointed directly at the fading shape of the Tardis.

The creature now lowered its shiny, insect-like head until it was peering through a sight mounted on the barrel – a sight shaped like a small web.

A chirruping noise came suddenly, shrilly, from a near-by crag where the twin eye-lights of another creature glowed. As if this were a signal, the creature aiming the cylinder- gun moved a foreleg suddenly, slamming home a plunger in the rear of the barrel.

Immediately the coiled glass sleeve around the barrel glowed and crackled into life.

As it did so the shape of Tardis, which had all but melted and vanished among its surroundings, returned and grew more solid.

Its motors whirred frantically, and in response the shape of the ship again began to fade. A concerted chirruping sound echoed around among the crags where a number of pairs of eyes now shone. The gun aimed at Tardis glowed more brightly, its crackling drowning the chirruping of the companion creatures on the crags surrounding the ship.

The motors of Tardis, throbbing furiously to clear the ship from this place, faltered, failed. Its police-box outlines now materialized clearly until it cast its own shadow.

Doctor Who and his three earth companions all heard the change in the sound of Tardis' motors as their powerful whir-ring faltered. Barbara and Vicki stared at each other in dismay.

A new sound now rose over the faltering of the ship's machinery – a high-pitched humming, speckled with a loud chirruping, and as it grew in volume Vicki screamed. She covered her ears and shut her eyes tightly against the pain of it. Barbara, too, gasped and clutched her temples, pressing her own ears to keep out its piercing, knife-sharp insistence.

Suddenly the whole ship lurched to one side. Ian and the Doctor grabbed at the control table to steady themselves, but the sudden jolt caught Vicki, who reeled away and fell sprawling on the floor where she lay writhing and moaning, still clasping her ears.

The shock hurled Barbara across the floor in the direction of the scanner. Now the ship settled and was still. She looked up. The scanner screen was again a mass of dazzling interference, the blobs of light speckling and bursting on it like millions of exploding lamps

As suddenly as it started, the humming with its overlay of shrill chirruping faded again. The crackling of interference on the scanner ceased. The motors, too, faltered finally and were still.

All was quiet again – uncannily quiet, now.

Ian released his grip on the control table and looked around him.

'That noise – I heard it too this time! Did you?'

'Yes,' Barbara said. 'I certainly did.' She took her hands from her ears wonderingly.

Doctor Who did not answer. He was furiously busy now, trying the motor switches. With a gesture of disgust he slammed the control table with his hand.

'No use! The response is nil.'

Barbara was looking up at the scanner . . . It had cleared completely of interference now, and its neighbouring inspection window now showed the planet's terrain surrounding them clearly.

Suddenly she cried, 'Ian, Doctor – look!'

Ian joined her, staring up at the inspection window. Doctor Who, with a final glance at his controls, followed.

'Well?' Ian said.

'I saw a light – out there. It came from behind one of those crags.'

Ian stared more closely. He shook his head unbelievingly. 'Where? I can't see anything.'

'I tell you, I saw it flash! It came from the top of that crag on the extreme left of the scanner!'

There was a pause while both Ian and Doctor Who studied the window. Finally Ian said 'Well it's not there now.'

'I can see it isn't – *now!*' Barbara said sharply. 'But *I saw it!*'

Doctor Who put up a soothing hand. 'All right, all right, no need for us to snap at each other.'

'Very well, but . . .'

'. . . what you saw, my dear', Doctor Who said gently, 'was most probably cosmic interference. The picture broke up.'

'But the screen was clear when it happened. The landmark were distinctly visible. I'm . . . almost sure . . .'

Ian had turned away. He saw Vicki still sprawled on the floor, but rising feebly on one elbow now, dazed and a little tearful as her senses returned. He moved swiftly over to her, knelt, and gently helped her up. Vicki was wide-eyed now, a memory returning of the awful sound she had heard.

'It's . . . gone again' . . . she whispered.

Barbara came and helped Ian with her. She put an arm around Vicki and nodded towards the dormitory section.

'Yes, it's all right now, Vicki. I think you'd better have a lie down.'

Barbara slid open the dormitory section door and Vicki allowed herself to be led towards her bunk.

Ian turned to Doctor Who. He spared a glance for the dead landscape showing in the inspection window and looked at the control dials, now all wavering near their zero marks. Ian tried to sound light-hearted but he couldn't keep the grimness out of the look he passed to the Doctor.

'There *is* some force, then – out there.' He waved at the scanner. 'And we're stuck with it.'

Doctor Who pondered the scanner, straightened, and said briskly, 'Nothing for it, my boy, but to explore this place. Determine what this, um, interference is, and – how to counteract it.'

Ian sighed gloomily. From the sight of the planet on the screen, the prospect was not attractive. He nodded.

'Be right with you – I'll just tell the girls.'

Ian moved towards the dormitory door. Doctor Who turned back and stared thoughtfully at his control panel, stroking his chin, muttering uneasily to himself.

Barbara was coming out of the dormitory section. Ian nodded towards Vicki's bunk beyond the sliding door.

'How is she?'

He smiled now at her, and Barbara forgot the irritation she had felt with him.

'Better.' She turned. 'Doctor, do we have such a thing as a, well, a sedative?'

Doctor Who roused himself from glumly staring at his controls.

'Eh? Oh, should be with the first-aid kit, over there, in one of the cupboards.'

He pointed to a small movable table housing the astral computer. Barbara nodded, crossed to the table, began searching. Intent as she was on finding a medicine for Vicki, she seemed to have forgotten their plight in the ship, marooned and powerless on a bleak and alien planet.

Ian took a deep breath and resolved to tell her now what he and the doctor planned to do. Exploring this planet in search of whatever had wrecked the ship's controls, and now held them tight, would mean leaving the two girls alone in *Tardis* – unprotected.

He said, 'Barbara?'

'Just a minute, Ian.'

Barbara was opening doors and drawers in the astral computer table, rummaging for the first-aid kit. She clicked her tongue in disgust.

'Tch-tch. Look at all this stuff!' She had pulled out a mixture of tools, boxes of wire, valves, and some specimen cases containing souvenirs of various planets and the civilizations they had visited. At length she found the first-aid kit. 'Ah!' She paused, turned and looked accusingly across at Doctor Who. 'One of these days, Doctor, I'm going to have a big spring-clean around here, I promise you.'

Doctor Who grunted, absorbed with a problem. Ian stopped Barbara as she took a pill from a box and started back towards the dormitory.

'Barbara, the Doctor and I are going to have a look round – outside.'

Barbara halted and stared at him. An anxious look clouded her face. She flashed a look across towards Doctor Who and opened her mouth to protest. Ian added hastily, 'Don't worry – I'll see he doesn't wander too far away.'

'Well . . .', Barbara said uneasily.

Doctor Who got up abruptly and barked, 'Ready, Chesterton?'

Ian gave Barbara a reassuring smile and turned.

'Right,' he said briskly.

Barbara hesitated. She glanced at the grim landscape surrounding them which showed steadily now in the inspection window, then at both men. Her voice was a little uncertain.

'Uh, well . . . be careful, both of you.' She cleared her

throat and smiled at them. But she could not prevent herself from taking another fearful look at the scanner.

'Yes, yes,' Doctor Who said cheerfully. 'Of course. Chesterton?'

Ian moved to join the Doctor. Barbara halted, watching them, then straightened and went back to the dormitory. Doctor Who pressed the exit door button on the control panel and, staring thoughtfully, waited for the ship's door to slide open.

He was answered by a whirring sound, but the exit doors remained shut. Doctor Who flashed a look at Ian, frowned, and poised a finger to jab the exit button again – when the doors suddenly started to slide open, as if on their own accord.

It was Ian's turn to look puzzled. The Doctor masked his uneasy surprise.

'Delay in the circuit, probably,' he muttered.

Ian nodded and strode towards the now open exit. On the threshold, he turned. Doctor Who was still staring thoughtfully at the doors, muttering to himself.

'Doctor?'

'Yes, yes, my boy – coming . . .'

Doctor Who squared himself uncertainly and marched towards the open doors.

Ian stepped out.

Doctor Who followed him, staring about.

The ship's doors slid closed behind them.

Vicki raised herself on her bunk as Barbara came in, filled a glass, and offered it to her – together with a pill.

'Take that and you'll feel much better.'

'What is it?' Vicki said suspiciously. She loathed pills.

'It'll just help you sleep easier, that's all.'

Vicki shrugged, took the pill, closed her eyes, and swallowed it, sipping the water. Barbara sat on the edge of her bunk.

'That was quite a fall you took. No aches or pains?'

'No. My ears still sting a bit – but that's all.'

'Try and get some rest. You're a nervous sleeper. You were

tossing and turning all the time during your last sleep period.'

Vicki remembered. 'I was dreaming,' she said thoughtfully. 'Yes – I dreamed about . . . that sound! Before I ever really heard it.'

'Well, you can forget about it now. The pill should take care of that.'

Barbara absently pushed a bracelet back up her arm. The bracelet had slipped to her wrist. It was of heavy gold, with an incised pattern of laurel branches and a worn Latin inscription. It caught Vicki's eye.

'How lovely. I haven't seen you wear it before.'

'The bracelet?' I haven't had it all that long . . .'

'Was it a present?' Vicki asked. She turned the bracelet on Barbara's arm to look at the pattern.

'Yes.'

'From – Ian?' Vicki asked, faintly sly.

Barbara smiled at her curiosity. 'No. As a matter of fact it's from the Emperor Nero.'

'Oh, pull the other leg!'

Barbara shrugged. 'Please yourself.'

'How? When?'

Barbara got up. 'Maybe I'll tell you about it when you wake up. Not before.'

'Very well,' Vicki said. 'I'll ask Ian.'

'Then you'll have to wait. He and the Doctor are . . . looking around.'

Vicki started up, staring. 'You mean – they've gone *outside*? Into that dreadful place?'

'Now hush! They've promised not to go far. They're just trying to find out what it is that made the motors fail. Do try and get some sleep.'

Vicki sank back, her eyes clouded with doubt. Barbara watched her a moment. The young girl's eyes began to close, sleepily now, and Barbara pulled her blanket up to her chin.

Then she tiptoed out of the dormitory through the sliding doors into the control room, past the control table, and paused before the inspection window.

Through it she could make out the figures of Doctor Who

21

and Ian as they paused near a crag, then went on slowly, looking all round them, until the gloom of the place swallowed them from the scanner's sight.

Barbara turned back to the control table, and as she did so, her arm jerked strangely, as if of its own accord, and the gold Roman bracelet on it glittered in the light from the control panel. She halted and gave a startled gasp. She felt her arm and smiled. It was no wonder that she had a nervous twitch, after the strange events of the past hour.

Then her bracelet arm jerked again, strongly – so strongly that she could not resist its pull. A fearful half-scream rose in her throat.

She stifled it and wheeled around nervously, as if expecting to see someone else in the control room. But the control room was silent and empty.

A little panicky now, Barbara backed towards the sliding dormitory doors.

'Barbara?'

The call came from Vicki, but it startled Barbara and made her turn. Vicki stood in her bare feet at the door, wide-eyed at the sight of her.

'Oh, I'm sorry. Did I wake you, Vicki?'

'I thought I heard you call out.' Vicki said. 'Did you?'

Barbara hesitated. 'No, no. You shouldn't have got out of bed.'

'Aren't the others back yet?' Vicki yawned.

'Not yet.'

Vicki took another shrewder look at Barbara. 'Something *is* wrong – isn't it?'

'No! No . . .'

Barbara forced a smile. She rubbed her arm and sat down. Vicki was still looking at her. The younger girl said accusingly, 'You're nervous *too*. Like a cat on hot bricks!'

Barbara shrugged. 'It's just . . . something about this planet . . .'

Vicki yawned again. 'Uhuh . . . now why can't we materialize in some really *lovely* place? . . . at some truly wonderful time in its life among the stars . . . with lots of beautiful things to buy ... gorgeous clothes to wear ... splendid things to eat ... and marvellous people to meet and talk with ...' She paused at the sight of Barbara rubbing her arm. 'Your arm – is it hurting you?'

Clearly Barbara could not keep up her pretence that nothing strange had happened. She smiled and explained lightly, as though it were nothing ...

'Sounds silly, I know, but it feels as though ... my arm doesn't belong to me. A moment ago – it moved. All on its own, without my intending it to.'

She tried to keep it matter-of-fact, but Vicki stared. Barbara forced a laugh.

'There's probably a perfectly sensible explanation. It's only the things we don't understand that scare us.'

But Vicki was still staring, wide-eyed at this story. Then she turned to look around the control room, and up at the inspection window.

'Doctor Who ... Ian – I can't see them out there!'

'They're not far away. Now look – I thought you were going to catch up on your sleep.'

Vicki nodded obediently and turned back towards the dormitory. Barbara watched her go. The doors closed and suddenly, in the deathly still of the control room, she felt very alone. It seemed chill. She shivered.

Doctor Who and Ian had walked some fifty yards now from the police-box shell of *Tardis*. In the uncanny stillness, their footsteps crunched loudly on the terrain, which was like pebbly glass. Doctor Who came to a crag, bent close, peered at its base.

Ian halted and stared about him, listening, watchful, and uneasy.

The Doctor reached and pulled away a loose piece of rock. He turned, showed it to Ian. The rock, too, was glassy and shone.

'See this, Chesterton? Looks like mica – or one of the Silicates. I'd say it's capable of withstanding great heat.' His voice echoed weirdly in the still air.

Ian said abruptly, 'Listen!'

Doctor Who jerked up his head a little irritably at the interruption.

'You heard that, Doctor?'

'Now don't *you* start that nonsense, confound it! Heard *what*?'

But the Doctors protests died as Ian, still listening, raised a finger for silence. Now they both heard it again. It came back almost as his original voice, hollowly.

'. . . -ound it . . . heard *what*? . . . heard what . . . heard what? . . .'

The echo trailed away, repeating itself. Doctor Who exploded impatiently.

'Is that *all*? My dear boy, it's just an echo! You behave as if it's the first one you've ever heard.'

Ian was still listening to the fresh echoes of Doctor Who's voice. They rang and swooped among the crags. He shook his head and muttered, 'Of course not. But never an echo quite like that . . . Besides . . .' He shrugged.

'What is it?'

Ian looked about him. 'Just a feeling,' he said.

Doctor Who sniffed, stared again at the glassy piece of rock. 'What of?' He said testily.

'Well – of being watched . . .'

'Oh, good heavens! If there were any life here, naturally it would be curious about strangers appearing in its midst, wouldn't it? As it is, I see nothing. Not a thing! Now come on!'

And the Doctor dropped the glassy rock and strode forward again, staring keenly around him at the strange landscape formation, the shimmering ground, at the satellites which hung pale and motionless in the sky. Their footsteps echoed with startling loudness.

The shape of another crag loomed up ahead of them in the twilight gloom. Doctor Who was about to proceed on around it when Ian gripped his arm. He pointed upward silently.

This was no crag.

As their gaze took it all in they saw that this tall column of rock had not been fashioned by time and weather, like the other crags. It had a shape, a design.

Ian breathed, 'This was built!'

It was a statue, gigantically tall. Doctor Who was taking it all in.

'So it was ... Mm!'

The enormous rock was roughened by erosion and its weird design was barely visible on its shadow side. All that survived of its massive outlines made it appear like a huge totem pole of a figure not unlike a man's, with giant wings,

ribbed and folded, and with the remains of its upper limbs crossed on its chest.

The statue had a face of sorts, as scarred as a Sphinx ... two great holes that might have been eyes ... and a slit for a mouth. It stared unseeingly out across the desolate planet from high above them.

'Then there *is* life here – to have built that thing!'

'. . . or *was*,' Doctor Who corrected him, looking about. 'It's old, Chesterton. In these conditions, it might have been made a million years ago.' He stared upward. 'Pity we didn't bring a ladder with us. We might get a clearer idea of what it was.'

Ian laughed a little nervously. 'Well it's not Nelson, for sure.'

Doctor Who smiled, agreed. 'No. No pigeons. Still – that isn't what's holding the ship here . . . come on . . .'

'Right.'

This time it was Ian who took the lead. They came round the base of the great statue and there Ian halted again.

A round pool of liquid shone dully in the ground ahead of them. It was small, only a few paces across. A mist wreathed slowly upward from it.

Ian called, 'Doctor? Here . . .!'

He pointed and went on to the brink of the pool. He looked down at it and called back, 'I suppose it could be water? Any type of life would need that.'

And he stooped to gather up the liquid in both hands.

Doctor Who yelled, 'Chesterton – wait!'

Ian paused and the old man came rushing forward as if panicked by something. He thrust Ian aside from the pool so roughly that he staggered and almost fell.

'What's the matter?'

Doctor Who ignored him. He bent over the pool, stared down into it, then held out a hand and clicked his fingers.

'Your tie – that'll do . . . let me have your tie.'

'My tie?' Ian said, gaping a little.

'Quickly man, come on!'

Ian shrugged and removed the tie around his neck. Doctor Who snatched it without a word, held it up in his hand, and poised it over the misty pool.

'Now let's see . . .' he murmured.

Ian shouted an alarmed protest. 'What are you doing? Hey . . .!'

Doctor Who might have gone deaf, for he took no notice.

Instead he slowly lowered the tie into the pool, absorbed and intent, while Ian goggled.

As the tie dipped into the milky water of the pool a thick smouldering arose on the surface around it. The fumes drifted across and caught sharply at Ian's throat. He coughed and stared. Doctor Who dipped the tie deeper, waited, and then pulled it out. He turned and displayed this triumphantly to Ian.

The lower end of the tie had completely gone, eaten away, leaving only a frayed and smouldering remnant.

Ian choked, partly in fury, partly from the fumes still rising from the pool.

'Well, of all the . . .!' he spluttered.

'You see?' Doctor Who said simply.

'You . . . you've *ruined* it! That's my Coal Hill School tie! And you – you just . . .'

'. . . I just what? Saved your life! You were about to put your hands in it, were you not?' Doctor Who gestured towards the pool. 'There could have been the remains of a Coal Hill School *teacher* in there, instead of just his tie . . .'

The Doctor offered the remnant of Ian's tie back with a lofty disdain. Ian snatched at it furiously. Doctor Who snorted, 'Water, indeed! Water! What *did* they teach you at that school – apart from that ridiculous pastime of kicking a bladder about on a field? Mm?'

Ian shrugged. He had to grin. 'Ah well,' he said, and flung the rest of his tie into the pool, and watched it smoulder and vanish. Doctor Who chuckled, dug him consolingly in the ribs, wheeled, and took a couple of thoughtful paces away from the pool. He halted and stared around him at the strange landscape, pondering.

'Silica . . .' he muttered. 'Interference . . . possibly electronic? . . . and now . . . acid. Similar properties to formic acid, I shouldn't wonder. Strange . . . very strange . . .'

His voice trailed away into a mutter.

Ian watched the smouldering thinning away on the pool and roused himself to proceed on their exploration of this place.

As he did so, the head and shining eyes of a great ant-like creature appeared from behind a rock on the crag overlooking the pool.

It stared down at Ian and Doctor Who, both unaware of its presence.

Ian turned. The creature moved, vanished. A fragment of rock rolled from its place and fell.

Ian checked suddenly and stared more closely back at the pool. A ripple broke its surface and spread sluggishly towards him. He paused, his attention frozen, and yelled, 'Doctor – quickly!'

'Eh?'

'There's something in there! I saw a light – then something broke the surface!'

Doctor Who joined him, staring sceptically at the now still surface, and sniffed disbelievingly.

'A light?' The Doctor looked around them and snorted. 'Reflection of one of those planets, most likely . . .'

'I tell you I *saw* it! There were two lights, close together . . . down in that pool. Then something broke the surface – a sort of . . . claw, or something.'

Doctor Who was eyeing Ian stonily.

'Chterterton, if this is your idea of a prank, because of that tie business, it's a pretty childish one—'

'I tell you, *I saw something moving!*'

'In a pool of acid like that? Impossible! Come on!'

But Ian stood his ground, watching for further signs of life from the pool. Doctor Who flared impatiently.

'We've left those girls alone in *Tardis* to find the source of this interference! I suggest we put our minds to that!'

Doctor Who moved off. Ian turned unwillingly away from the pool to follow him.

Then they both halted. Out of the stillness among the crags both of them heard a sound. It was a low throbbing, which rose quickly to a steady humming. The brittle crags took up the sound as it grew. The humming rose in pitch until it was echoing all around them. Now, as it swelled to deafening proportions, a high-pitched chirruping joined the sound and pierced their ears.

Both men stared around them tensely, listening. The noise was so shrilly intense now that it hurt their ears.

Yet not a thing around them moved.

The noise was everywhere. Inside *Tardis'* control room Barbara had heard it, paused in her watch on the inspection screen, and stiffened. The sound boomed around her as if the control room had become one vast echo chamber.

Barbara backed towards the dormitory, slid the door aside to retreat from the sound, then with a glance towards the sleeping Vicki, changed her mind.

Vicki stirred in her sleep, and moaned.

Barbara closed the door on her and turned, trapped. The humming grew louder, speckled now with a high-pitched chirruping. She stared towards the screen in hopes of seeing the comforting figures of Ian and the Doctor in the distance, out among the crags on the planet, but the inspection window was black. Then something caught her eye.

The control table to the right of the ship's doors moved – visibly. A metal food canister on the table's surface jumped – then fell back with a clatter. Its lid dislodged and fell on to the floor, spinning away into a corner and rolling to a stop.

The control table turned, slowly at first, then spun, violently. A ruler and several containers whirled off it on to the floor and scattered loudly.

Barbara gasped and instinctively moved to halt the table and gather the fallen containers – but she could not budge. It felt as though her feet were suddenly glued to the floor. She remained, back to the dormitory door, frozen now with fear.

As she stood there her arm jerked abruptly – out of her own control. She gave a little scream and tried to pull her hand back to her side but it remained immovable, pointing towards the ship's exit doors.

A moan of terror died on her lips. She caught her breath quickly as, slowly, the ship's doors slid open.

'What . . . what's happening?' she whispered.

Beyond the doors she could see the shadowy crags and a pale gleam of light on the brittle ground of this strange planet.

The humming and the chirruping now rose to fever pitch, and with it Barbara's face clouded slowly and her eyes grew blank.

Dully, like a sleepwalker, with her arm still held out before her, she began to move.

She took a reluctant step towards the door, then another. The gold of the Roman bracelet glittered on her outstretched arm. She moved on stiffly and did not even pause as she went out of the now open doors.

Without looking around her, and with her face now blank, empty of expression, Barbara stepped on out and walked dreamily forward into the gloom of the planet.

The ship's doors whirred quietly and slid closed behind her.

As they did so the humming and the high-pitched chirruping which overlaid it faded. It seemed impossible to believe that such a total silence could follow such all-enveloping sounds. But now, as a container lid ceased spinning on the floor and settled after a final clatter, the control room was ghostly quiet. The control table had ceased spinning and stood solid and motionless.

In the dormitory Vicki had been turning in a troubled sleep, moaning, her face puckered and strained.

It was the abrupt silence which suddenly woke her. She sat up and listened.

'Barbara?' she murmured.

The dormitory door to the control room was closed.

'Barbara?' she called louder.

There was no answer, no sound from the other room.

Vicki threw aside her blanket and got up. Sleepily she slid aside the door and came into the control room.

It was empty. She peered into the corners. The scatter of metal containers across the floor caught her eye.

Again she called, 'Barbara!'

Suddenly a terror seized her too. Wildly she looked at the scanner, then at the closed exit doors.

She screamed, 'Where are you?'

The control room only threw back the panic sound of her own voice.

Vicki stared about her again. She was alone in the ship. Doctor Who, Ian and Barbara had now all left it!

She lunged towards the control table and pressed the exit button. A quiet whirring answered her, and they opened.

Vicki ran to the door and peered out fearfully. The landscape with it sinister towering crags, harsh and empty in the ghostly light, gave back no sign of life, no sound now.

Vicki was afraid to break this chilly silence, but then her fear of being alone overcame all other thought.

'Barbara!' she screamed. 'Barbara . . .!'

Doctor Who and Ian listened, but the roaring hum and the strange chirruping that had risen with it had now vanished utterly, so that when Ian took a pace forward, his step echoed again. He halted, straining his ears.

'Where did it come from?'

Doctor Who remained where he was, listening too. The Doctor wagged his head, frowning thoughtfully.

'It's . . . it's some form of communication. I'm sure of it . . .'

Ian turned his head swiftly back. 'Are you saying those noises we heard were *messages*?'

A slow nod. A pause.

'They come from some sentient thing . . . or, . . . perhaps, a machine operated by it.'

Suddenly Doctor Who stopped as though struck by an idea.

'Of course!'

He looked up at the crags, around him, then stared triumphantly at Ian.

'That's what's holding us here!'

'This . . . sound?' Ian said, puzzled.

'Whatever's making it . . . yes! Aurally it's the same

pattern. The same pulse, the same rhythm as we got on the scanner.'

'Those bars of light, those blobs . . . all that interference!' The Doctor gripped Ian's arm. 'Chesterton, we've got to locate its source!'

Ian hesitated. 'Yes . . . but how? With all those echoes around us? It could have come from anywhere! Trying to trace it would be hopeless!'

'It isn't,' the Doctor snapped. 'Not if we use one of our detectors. Come on – let's get back to the ship . . .!'

He turned to retrace his steps. Ian pointed to a defile between the crags.

'It's this way, Doctor'.

He led on. As they entered the defile another distant sound floated to them over the crunching of their boots. Ian was first to hear it and stayed Doctor Who with his hand. They paused and it floated to them again, a faint anxious echo.

'. . . Barbara . . . Barbara . . .!'

'It's Vicki!' Ian shouted. 'Something's wrong, back at the ship!'

'I thought you told them not to leave it?'

'I did! Come *on*, Doctor!'

Ian raced ahead, stumbling over the uneven ground, charging blindly down the defile. It was the Doctor who saw the danger which loomed suddenly ahead of them both, and halted.

Illuminated palely in this cold light something was stretched between two tall rocks across the defile, barring their way. It glittered faintly.

It was a web – a giant one, swaying faintly between the crags. Ian, stumbling ahead, turned to yell over his shoulder.

'Hurry, Doctor!'

'Chesterton! In front of you! Look out!'

But Ian had turned to race on and came charging straight into the immense web. Its threads enveloped him stingingly wherever they touched. Ian thrust out his hands and clawed wildly to free himself, but the web caught his hands too, and

32

prickled wherever they touched bare flesh. He saw Doctor Who running towards him as he fought vainly to free himself.

'Keep away, Doctor! Get back to the ship!'

His further shouts were drowned in the humming that now again rose all around them, speckled with the curious insect chirruping. He yelled again desperately, as Doctor Who halted a little helplessly.

'Get back to the ship!'

But Doctor Who stood there, warily free of the great mesh of the glistening web.

'Don't move! Stay absolutely still!' the Doctor commanded.

'It hurts!' Ian gasped. 'It . . . stings . . .!'

'Don't move, I say!'

Ian ceased his struggling. He winced at the strands of the web which lay stingingly across his face. Doctor Who was peering at the web for all the world as if it was a specimen of great scientific interest. He reached out a wary hand, touched it, and drew immediately back.

'Hmmm!' he grunted. 'No good – I'll have to go back to *Tardis* – get something to free you with.'

'. . . all . . . right . . .'

'Now keep as still as you can! I'll try not to be too long!'

Ian managed a faint nod. The web strands which held him powerless prickled even through his coat-sleeves and across his chest.

Doctor Who backed away, took his bearings, and looking cautiously around him, circled the crag.

Vicki gasped and backed away, clutching her ears as the noise invaded the ship again and pierced her ears like a knife. As she stumbled backward into the control room, the exit doors whirred and closed.

The ship gave a sudden lurch. She shrieked and put out her hands to grab the control panel. The whole room tilted to one side. She held on desperately as the ship lurched again, and looked wildly up at the inspection window.

Tardis seemed to be moving!

The whole control room tilted and jerked with its slow movement, and in answer to it the view of the dark landscape outside through the inspection window, now clearing, tilted crazily this way and that.

In her terror Vicki flicked desperately at the switches on the control table, pausing only for an agonized moment to press her ears against the intolerable noise that rumbled and chirruped all around her.

The control column glowed in response to a switch and began moving up and down.

But no other controls answered. The ship lurched again. Scraping sounds came from its hull. Yes, it was moving all right! Through the inspection window the crags moved slowly passed, tilting jerkily as the ship scraped and slithered forward.

Breathing heavily, Doctor Who climbed painfully around rocks and paused, seeking a new path back to where *Tardis* lay. He had made a circuit of the defile and ahead of him he recognized the circle of crags and the bare, dead surface on to which they had emerged to explore this planet.

He came hurrying and stumbling down towards it, puffing a little, peering this way and that around him.

He slithered down on to smoother ground, halted, came forward, and stared about.

At first he thought he was mistaken.

But the image of this place, which he had first seen through the inspection screen was etched unmistakably on his mind.

There was no doubt about it. This was the spot where they had first stepped out of *Tardis*.

He was standing almost on the actual site where the ship had been.

Doctor Who stared around him and passed a trembling hand over his brow.

'The ship!' he muttered. 'It's . . . *gone!*'

CHAPTER TWO

The Zarbi

Barbara walked slowly onward as if in a trance. She seemed unconscious of the deafening hum which resounded echoingly all around her. Her eyes were fixed glassily ahead. She stumbled unseeingly, but rose and came on, her arm still outstretched before her as though it were pulling her forward.

She did not even see the peril ahead of her.

Right in her path glimmered an acid pool, giving off its slow, vaporous mist.

She came slowly but directly towards the pool, seemingly drawn by it. Her steps came nearer and nearer, yet still she did not look down, or appear aware of it.

Then a light shone from a near-by crag and the fore-quarters of one of the huge shiny creatures inhabiting this place reared its shape against the sky. Its luminous eyes glared downward and abruptly it raised a glistening fore-claw.

Barbara was now at the brink of the pool. It seemed certain that her next pace or so would carry her into its unseen depths. It shone sullen and still, seeming harmless except for the faint acid fumes drifting up from its murky surface.

She made as if to step forward, then halted abruptly.

The creature above moved its claw, describing a circle with it.

At that Barbara obediently turned. Slowly she skirted the pool, her bracelet arm still held before her, and walked on, wide-eyed but unseeing.

The prickly sting of the great web which held Ian fast was becoming unbearable. At length he could stand it no longer. He lunged forward in a desperate attempt to burst free, but the web's merciless strands only gripped him tighter and

stung more deeply through his clothes and on his bare face
and hands.

Above the noise of the humming around him he heard a
slithering on rocks and Doctor Who scrambled into sight.

The Doctor picked himself up and came wearily forward,
shaking his head.

He halted, opened his bare hands in a helpless gesture, and
said simply, 'The *Tardis* has gone!'

Ian stopped his tormented struggling.

'What do you mean, *gone*?'

Doctor Who grunted testily and searched about him. He
spied and picked up a slender spar of fallen silica rock.

'I thought I said it plainly enough. It's not there, Chesterton. Not where we left it. It's vanished!'

The Doctor raised the thin spar of rock, gritted his teeth,

swung and slashed at the great web around Ian with it. The strands parted under the impact.

'Hold still, for goodness sake!'

Doctor Who swung at the air above Ian's head, cleaving through more of the stinging strands, until Ian burst from its weakening grip – and broke free, rubbing his smarting face and hands.

Doctor Who had picked up a glistening thread of the web with the tip of the spar and was examining it gingerly.

'Mm . . . no wonder it stung. Look – statically charged!'

Sure enough, though Doctor Who waved the spar about, the severed strand clung to it like steel to a magnet.

Ian leaned weakly against a rock, brushing off the remaining barbs of web which clung to him. The Doctor had become so absorbed in his find that he seemed to have forgotten all else.

'This is no natural phenomenon,' he murmured, mostly to himself. 'It's not a plant, nor a . . .'

Ian interrupted him, terse and impatient.

'All right – so somebody put it there! But what about *Tardis*?'

Doctor Who now stood back and surveyed the remains of the great web with an air of profound interest.

'Yes,' he said. 'Something with a *brain*! It makes those sounds. And it made . . . that!'

'Doctor, for heaven's sake, we've got to get back to where the ship was! Find out what's happened to it!'

Doctor Who roused himself. 'Mm? Oh – yes . . .'

With a last pensive look at the web, Doctor Who followed Ian. This time they both kept a wary look-out, halting to listen now and then for the source of the hum that rose and faded among the crags, keeping an eye open to avoid blundering into any such trap as the web which had caught Ian.

As he hurried on, stumbling occasionally over loose rock, the thought came to Ian that the web he had run into had not been there on the journey outward. They had come this same way, through this same defile.

37

Something must have drawn it, or spun it, between those two crags, while they were examining the acid pool. To bar their retreat?

They emerged from the defile into the familiar clearing between the crags. Ian waited for Doctor Who to join him. The old man caught up, puffing and muttering at the pace the younger man had set.

They stared around.

Sure enough, the clearing was empty. The humming had receded to a point where they thought they could fix its direction.

Behind the stalagmite shapes of a cluster of distant crags there was a faint glow, low in the sky. Ian touched Doctor Who's arm and pointed.

'It's coming from over there – isn't it? Is that a light?'

Doctor Who studied the horizon. After a moment he shook his head.

'No. Reflection of a satellite, I imagine. But I do agree, now that the echo has gone . . . it does seem to be coming from that quarter.'

Doctor Who returned to musing over the disappearance of the *Tardis*, stroking his chin and shaking his head.

'There *must* be a simple answer, Chesterton! They couldn't have got it working, let alone operate it . . .'

'Who – the girls, you mean?' Ian muttered. He was inspecting the ground closely all around them. A furrow in the glassy sand caught his eye. He stooped and walked, tracing it a way. He straightened.

'Doctor? Over here . . .!'

Ian pointed downward and Doctor Who came up.

'It's been dragged away – look!'

At this point beyond the reaching shadows of the crags there was a wide furrow in the ground between the scattered rock.

'And tracks . . . see? There . . . and there . . . good Lord, there are dozens of them!'

Doctor Who bent and peered. All around the furrow a multitude of strange imprints cast faint shadows in the dim, slanting light.

The tracks were single, narrow and deep. They pitted the ground on either side of the deeper furrow marks, and although the light was too pale to show where they ended they led away in an almost straight line, out of the clearing circled by the crags.

Ian was down on one knee, staring more closely at them. 'What kind of thing could have made those?'

Doctor Who shrugged. '. . . Interesting, isn't it?' he said.

'Interesting! Doctor, the ship has *gone* – and the girls with it!'

He straightened and faced the absent old man.

'Doctor Who, *where are we?* What is this place? Have you no idea at all?'

Doctor Who was looking through and beyond him, staring into a remoteness of his own.

'It can't be,' he murmured. 'Yet it must be. These rock formations . . . silica . . . the planet . . . it's Vortis, surely . . .'

'Vortis? What's that?'

'But strangely . . . different from what one would expect. And these creatures . . . they *could* be . . . Zarbi. I wonder . . .' Doctor Who collected himself. 'Forgive me – I'm only guessing, really.'

'Then let's get on! Whatever these things are, they've got the ship!'

'M'yes . . . almost certainly . . .'

'Let's follow these tracks! Come on . . .!'

Stooping, peering to left and right, Ian led the way ahead, following the multitude of tracks.

'Carefully, Chesterton. Keep your eyes open.'

Ian nodded impatiently. 'This way . . . over here . . .'

They went on, tracking the numberless imprints in the glittering sand.

The crags closed around Barbara as she walked slowly on into a winding shadowy pass between them, where the humming and the echoes boomed and soared.

The glowing eyes of the creature on the crag which had guided her around the acid pools and onward, now turned to follow her progress as Barbara stepped further into the pass. The shadows from the peaks around it began to enclose her.

She blinked a little now, as if something within her was awakening and resisting the impulse to go on. She paused and looked about her, her eyes clearing faintly, and stepped more hesitantly forward.

As she rounded a tumble of rocks at the base of the silica cliffs a figure stepped out from the shadows behind her. It lunged and threw its winged arms around her throat.

Barbara gasped and struggled wildly but the enveloping arms choked off the terrified scream which rose in her throat . . .

Though it seemed like a nightmarish dream not happening to herself, she fought weakly to wrench herself free. Her resistance was leaden and without will. A shaft of pale light illuminated her attacker and its threshing, glistening wings, its strange ribbed body markings, its furry face with its small glittering eyes and its grim slash of a mouth.

The creature was lithe and quick. It clamped a leaf-shaped hand across her mouth and dragged her, writhing feebly, onwards towards an opening in the rock.

It was pulling her into a cave among the cliff-like crags. It relaxed its hold on her mouth, and another winged shape swooped from the darkness to join them, seizing her arm, dragging her further inward.

In her strange half-awake state she knew only a dull help-less fear and could summon no will of her own to fight. Only the weird force which had drawn her forth from the ship and brought her this far still pulled her on – against the attempts of these winged shadows wrenching at her, dragging her further into the cave under the towering rocks.

Dimly she saw the vile, misty pools that dotted the cave floor, and the small slender stalagmites which speared up-ward all around them towards the roof.

The faces of two more creatures, lurking in the cave shadows, loomed out of the darkness to peer at Barbara as she was pushed into a sitting position on a rock. One of the tall bat-like creatures held her there. The other three crowded closer, inspecting her, their small shiny eyes alive in furry faces, their leaf-shaped hands gripping brittle pointed sticks of stalagmite, like spears.

They stared at her wordlessly and looked towards the creature which held her. One reached out with the stalagmite stalk and stirred her hair curiously.

Gradually her captor released its grip. As it did so, Barbara, still dreamily obeying a magnet-like force which again lifted her braceleted arm, began to get up again.

At that one of the winged creatures acted swiftly. It snatched at Barbara's arm. With its delicate leaf-shaped hand, it wrenched off the heavy Roman bracelet and, holding it delicately as though it were lethal, hastily hurled it across the cave towards one of the smoking pools.

The bracelet plopped into the pool. Immediately there was a hissing, a bubbling which rose turgidly from its depths, and the ripples on the pool smouldered thickly. The sharp fumes caught at Barbara's throat and she coughed.

Her face cleared. Her eyes opened as she came out of her trance-like state.

She looked wonderingly around and instinctively felt her bare wrist. Sleepily she muttered.

'My bracelet . . . I . . . was . . .'

She looked up, around her, and it seemed that she saw for the first time. There was a tall sinister dignity about them – a beauty even, but with the sudden shock of their strange appearance and their glaring hostility, she felt the sickness of a real terror welling up inside her.

One of the creatures raised an arm, and with it, its wings unfolded, gaudy and shot with iridescent colours – green, lime yellow, streaks of brilliant scarlet – for all the world like a malignant butterfly.

Barbara shrank back and stammered wildly 'Who are you? What do you want?' Foolishly, she realized they could not possibly understand her – even though there was something about those stares they turned on her that was almost human.

Then her panic overwhelmed her. She turned, and scrambled blindly to her feet, and dived for the cave exit.

A voice rang hollowly after her in the cave.

'Stop! Stay where you are!'

One of the gaudy creatures lunged and barred her way, levelling a stalagmite spar like a sword at her.

Barbara stopped, frozen with amazement and fear. She turned. One of the creatures had *spoken!*

Its accent was strange, stilted, high-pitched, but the commanding words were clear, unmistakable.

Or was she still dreaming?

She flinched as the creature barring her escape prodded her with the glassy spar.

'Who . . . who . . . are you . . . ?' she whispered.

The voice came from the creature which appeared to be their leader. It came slowly forward; its long, slim, black body ribbed with glowing green shone in the uncertain light. The gorgeous wings folded as it lowered its delicate arms.

It spoke again. 'We are the Menoptera,' it said.

'Men . . . optera . . . ?' In her fear and amazement Barbara had difficulty with the word.

'Lords of Vortis.'

The Menoptera gestured to the landscape beyond the mouth of the cave and turned its intent glittering stare on Barbara. Its mouth closed harshly.

'How come you here?'

Barbara gathered the courage to speak but an angry movement from one of the surrounding Menoptera made her flinch back. Its voice crackled more harshly.

'Kill her, Vrestin! Now!'

It raised its stalagmite spar ready to thrust and impale her on its cruel point. The taller Menoptera raised a hand, stayed the blow with a commanding wave.

'First we speak!'

It paused, and in silence its burning gaze bored through Barbara. She mustered a calm and said, trembling a little, '. . . you . . . know our earth language? H-how . . . ?'

'*Answer* us only!' A pause, then – 'there are . . . more of you?'

'. . . er, yes . . . but . . .'

'More?'

'Four of us. But please – we mean no *harm*! We are peaceful, civilized. We have . . . lost our way . . . in space . . .'

Barbara halted lamely. The glaring scrutiny of four pairs of eyes on her was unrelenting, unmoved. One of the Menoptera creatures cast a nervous look back towards the cave mouth, and rounded angrily on the Menoptera it had addressed as 'Vrestin'.

'We are wrong to spare her. She must be killed – quickly!'

Vrestin raised a hand for silence. He turned to Barbara. His straight mouth opened and his stilted voice addressed her.

'You say you are lost. That there are three others.'

Barbara nodded. 'Yes, we . . .'

'. . . yet we found you – wandering alone. How?'

Barbara tried to think. She said, hesitating, 'I only know that . . . after we landed, two of our party went to explore, and . . .'

'Explore . . .!' A Menoptera repeated, hostile, scornful.

'. . . the last thing I remember was being in the ship, and the doors opening . . .'

Vrestin stared closely at her. 'Ship?'

'Yes. I . . . stayed aboard. But . . . something . . . made the doors open. All I can recall since then . . . is . . .' she gestured helplessly, '. . . is . . . well, I was here . . .'

The most hostile of the four Menoptera thrust forward and gripped the shoulder of the tall one they called Vrestin. 'We waste time and risk much! Kill her! Now!'

Vrestin hesitated. Another Menoptera came close. Its eyes studied her. Its voice was reedy, hoarse.

'You chose ill, when you chose to land on Vortis.'

'Hrostar is right!'

'We didn't *choose*!' Barbara cried. 'Our ship was *pulled* towards . . . this planet. We are helpless here!'

The Menoptera looked at each other.

The one called Hrostar spoke.

'If we let you go back to your ship . . .'

'No!' The other interrupted. 'A stranger must not be trusted!'

43

Their leader Vrestin shook his head too. 'The Zarbi will treat them as enemies. If we refuse our help they will not survive.'

'Their welfare is not our concern!' The most hostile of these creatures pointed the spar he held at Barbara. 'She was under the force of the Zarbi!' He rounded accusingly on Vrestin. 'What made you snatch her from them?'

Vrestin glared back at his glowering companion. 'Challis – should we all shrink back into the dark while such vile things as the Zarbi practise their power on ... civilized creatures?'

'The ... Zarbi?' Barbara asked. 'W-who ... are they, please?'

Hrostar stared suspiciously. 'You do not know them? You did not *see* them?'

Barbara shook her head timidly.

'The Zarbi have brought the Dark Age to Vortis,' Vrestin said simply. 'They have overrun it like a plague. And like a plague, they destroy every living thing in their path.'

The hostile Challis grew impatient. 'Vrestin, she is a danger to us!'

Vrestin nodded regretfully. 'I know.'

The finality with which he said that scared Barbara. His was the only kindly face which looked down upon her, and now it hardened. Vrestin turned, beckoning to the others.

'Please!' Barbara pleaded. 'We ... we only want to get away from here! These ... Zarbi you're afraid of – perhaps we can, well, – help you ...!

Challis sneered in amazement.

'You?'

'Our men have great gifts ... wisdom ... experience ... knowledge.'

Hrostar drew himself up haughtily. 'You dare to believe *you* can withstand the Zarbi? That your wisdom is greater than ours? The Menoptera are the greatest civilization this galaxy has known, yet the Zarbi swept it from this planet! Their power was invincible ...!'

'... they laid our greatness in ... ashes,' Vrestin added in a murmur.

44

Challis interrupted them, his high-pitched voice rising to a frenzied shriek. 'If we are to restore it, we cannot risk betrayal! Let her go and she will tell the Zarbi where they can find us!'

Vrestin and Hrostar considered that doubtfully.

'Please, I . . . promise I will not!' Barbara urged them.

'What are promises? They will extort it from her! And what proof have we of what she says? Killing her is the *only* answer!'

The fourth Menoptera, lingering in the background and keeping a watchful eye on the cave entrance, murmured his agreement.

Vrestin hesitated, inclined his head.

He said curtly, 'We shall decide the matter. Come. Challis, you will guard.'

The idea pleased the hostile Challis. He moved quickly and took up a grim stance with a spar levelled at Barbara's throat.

Vrestin signed to their other two companions and led them farther into the dark recesses of the cave. Challis pushed the spar at Barbara, motioning her roughly to sit.

From the rear of the cave Barbara could hear the murmur of their strange, almost flute-like voices. It was impossible to pick up what they were saying.

The guard, Challis, who towered over her, also turned his head for a brief cautious moment to listen, but returned immediately to watching her. Her mouth was dry with fear. Barbara racked her brains for a way of appealing to these creatures – winning some sign of friendliness, trust.

They used human speech. But did they have feelings akin to human beings? Did they know mercy?

In such a grim place as this, it did not seem possible. She shivered.

'Please – you *must* see that I am harmless!'

At that Challis raised the spar menacingly. Barbara braved it, but her voice quavered a little.

'We speak in the same way. We may have much in common that you can trust. At least let me . . .'

45

'. . . silence!' Challis snarled. He glared and thrust the spar until it was an inch from Barbara's mouth.

A commotion from the rear of the cave made them both turn their heads. The voices of the three Menoptera were raised in dispute, but Barbara could not catch more than one or two words, oddly distorted as they echoed off the brittle walls.

'. . . kill her . . . outright . . . and have done . . . the . . . Zarbi will . . .'

Barbara stared up at her captor. He glared back and then turned to listening, straining his ears. She cast around desperately, and her gaze lit on the rocks that glittered on the cave floor.

Slowly, so as not to excite Challis' attention, her hand strayed towards a rock. Her fingers gripped it, and then, desperately, as Challis turned back and saw the rock in her hand, she hurled it at his head.

Without waiting she whirled to her feet and raced for the cave mouth. As she did so she heard Challis give a shriek. Out of the corner of her eye she saw the creature reel back with a winged hand to his eyes. His stalagmite spar gleamed as it dropped and he screamed.

'Stop her!'

She ran, slipping and stumbling, her heart pounding wildly, towards the pale oval of light marking the cave mouth. Behind her she heard the shouts of the Menoptera as they came running from the rear of the cave towards their comrade Challis. Barbara leaped over a rock, came scrambling out of the cave mouth into the twilit pass and ran on till her breath gave out. She paused for a moment and leaned to catch her breath in the shadow of the cliffs. She threw a quick look back towards the cave mouth, then stared fearfully around her, wondering where the ship was. How would she find it? What direction should she take?

Barbara realized she had no idea, no memory of having walked through this place.

She was entirely lost and alone. She stared up at the craggy cliffs. Could she climb up there – find a vantage point from

46

which to see the land around her? The sides were too glassy, too steep.

As Barbara decided this, a sound checked her. It was something she had first heard in the control room of *Tardis*, and with its return the memory flooded back too.

It was fainter now, a humming, a chirruping.

But it was enough. Her mind flashed back to the chaos that awful sound had caused in the control room. She remembered the metal canisters jumping and scattering across the floor, the control table spinning wildly, how her own arm had jerked in front of her as though controlled by something else – and how the doors of *Tardis* had opened.

It was immensely evil – this sound.

Barbara gave a shriek and clapped her hands to her ears. She turned and ran blindly up the pass, no longer wondering where to go, obeying only the panic impulse to run from the great humming, to hide, to find somewhere blessedly silent, safe from it.

As she ran and stumbled along the rocky pass she turned her head wildly to the right and left as if expecting to see whatever was making the sound suddenly appear from the shadows and close in on her.

She checked and darted up a small gorge leading off the pass. There she halted and turned to run in a new direction.

But whichever way Barbara turned, the sound grew louder.

And now she could run no more. She was utterly spent. She simply dropped there, holding her aching sides, her heart pounding like a steam-hammer, fighting to get her breath.

As she straightened again, summoning the strength to go on, she saw clusters of light appear from behind the rocks in the gloom. Then to her right the hideous sleek shape of a Zarbi reared on its hind legs out of the gloom, glaring down, and with a slithering sound began to scramble towards her. The other lights converged and took shape too. The pass ahead of her and to her right was swarming with these loathsome creatures, and the chirruping sound they made, as they came crowding and slithering down towards her, bored echoingly through her head and vibrated on every nerve.

47

Barbara stopped stock-still and moaned, 'No . . . no . . . !'

She backed away into a small gorge, turned to run, but saw her retreat was cut off by a solid wall of rock.

She cowered back against it, eyes wide, mouth quivering, trembling all over with a cold sickness.

Two of the Zarbi loomed now right in front of her. Barbara pressed herself desperately into a crack in the rock. The leading Zarbi reached out with its great shiny foreleg.

Its pincer claws clamped like sharp steel on her arms.

She screamed, and the sound echoed off every crag.

There was chaos inside the control room of *Tardis*. It lurched and tilted in every direction, its hull scraping over rock and rough ground.

Vicki, alone in the ship, clung to the control table for support and ventured another look at the screen.

Through it, the landscape outside had lightened, and she saw what seemed to be ropes stretching far out ahead of the ship, ending in moving figures whose shapes she could not make out clearly.

Then a scuttling, slithering noise echoed above her head and she opened her mouth dumbly in terror at the object which now suddenly appeared at the inspection window.

Two giant, glaring eyes in a shiny, pointed head peered through the scanner window. The eyes, huge and distorted as through a great magnifying glass, stared inward, looking this way and that – then caught and held Vicki, and burned venomously right through her.

Vicki screamed and plunged for the switches on the control table to blot out the sight.

She thought she heard a strange high-pitched cry, then a slithering sound, as she fumbled haphazardly with the controls before finding the inspection off-switch.

The screen blanked out, but the ship went lurching on.

Outside the ship, a host of Zarbi swarmed around it. A great web had been spread over the exterior of its police-box shell, and from this a number of long, thin, rope-like strands, glittering like glass, radiated outward to a group of Zarbi, who toiled along, their shiny bodies reared upright, pulling steadily.

They looked for all the world like giant ants, gripping the strands between pincer claws and lurching along with their ungainly, slithering gait.

Their bodies were long and jointed in sections like an insect's – first the great shiny head with huge eyes and cruel proboscis jaw that moved and clamped together like the tips of an enormous tweezer; then a short trunk, dark, shiny, smooth, shell-like too; and finally the glistening swollen posterior which ended in a point like the sting-end of a bee. They moved on the hind pair of six steely legs, and now it was clear that the shrill chirruping which Doctor Who and the others had heard came from these creatures.

The Zarbi came lurching on now over rougher, rising ground till their leading Zarbi reached a ridge. Here they paused and turned to haul *Tardis* up with them, then rested.

One of the Zarbi turned its glaring eyes to look ahead. It chirruped faintly and extended a claw. Its companion at the head of the column joined it and followed the pointing foreclaw.

Beyond the ridge, in the centre of a great basin of land dotted with crags, a light shone, pulsating as it turned. The revolving light crowned the dome of a strange, sprawling structure whose spokes spread out like living creeper all over the land around, enveloping rocks and circling the bases of the crags.

The creeper, reaching and curling far outward from this building, glowed luminously.

The building itself was like a colossal, illuminated web, thick and dome-shaped at its core. The light pulsing at its very centre revolved again, its reflections glittering faintly on the shiny bodies of the watching Zarbi.

The leaders of the toiling column seized the tow strands in their claws and began moving down towards it.

It was growing harder for Ian and Doctor Who to follow the tracks of the ship and the prints around it. The glassy sand had given way to rocky ground, and here, gradually, the

furrow left by *Tardis* grew fainter. So did the strange marks
that had pitted the softer terrain over which they had come.

Finally the tracks petered out entirely and Ian halted,
scanning all around him for further marks.

'They've disappeared,' he said.

Doctor Who ground a foot into the flinty terrain. 'Mm –
hard as rock here. Still, we should pick up some marks. Have
a good look round.'

But Ian was worried. He stared at the landscape ahead of
them, then at Doctor Who.

'Doctor – what are we going to do when we *find* the ship?'

Doctor Who waved an impatient hand, peering all around
him intently. 'One thing at a time, Chesterton. Let's not cross
our bridges until we get to them. It's a waste of brain-power!'

'Yes, but – Barbara and Vicki . . .'

Doctor Who raised his head, glared and snapped, 'Do you
imagine I'm not thinking about them? Now start looking!
Start looking!'

He turned his attention to seeking tracks where the
smooth unyielding surface gave way again to a tumble of
glassy stone and jagged pebbles.

Ian watched him stepping gingerly away, the silvery head
peering alertly this way and that. He himself surveyed the
going ahead. The ground sloped downward and narrowed
into a pass between great outcrops of pointed rock. Ian
started towards it, placing his feet as delicately as a moun-
taineer on the polished, time-worn slope.

Was that a chirruping he heard, echoing somewhere ahead
of him in the distance?

Ian went on. The shadows of the pass folded around him
until he could hardly see the ground.

Then his foot crunched into something softer, a shape lying
on the ground.

It was not a rock. Ian bent and stared, and the hairs
prickled icily on the back of his neck. He pulled his foot
hurriedly away and shouted, 'Over here, Doctor!'

He turned back and looked again at the thing he had
stepped on.

A strange face, with holes where eyes might have been, stared sightlessly back at him from the shadowed ground. His foot had gone straight through its chest, crumbling it like a hollow shell.

Steps came slithering down towards him from behind, and Doctor Who bent and looked in the direction of Ian's pointing finger.

'What do you make of that, Doctor?'

The Doctor's eyes gleamed with interest as he stooped to study the shape. Suddenly Ian realized, staring down, what the crumbling body reminded him of.

'That great statue we saw back there – it was a figure of this . . . creature, surely? Look . . .'

He pointed. 'See where the wings were?'

'Indeed I do. Hm! Yes!'

'Then now we know at least what took *Tardis*! These creatures!'

Doctor Who knelt for a closer look. He shook his head. 'No,' he said, straightening. 'Those tracks we've been following are claw marks of some kind.'

'Well?'

Doctor Who indicated the lower part of the mummified figure.

'Take a close look at the feet. Not claws – in fact, almost like human feet. See?' He paused. 'No, I don't think it's this creature which has the ship.'

He bent again to examine the rest of the body.

'Hollow,' the Doctor murmured. 'Yet – preserved. A vertebrate creature, highly developed. Just the shell left. It makes sense, Chesterton. It . . . makes . . . sense . . .'

'How do you mean – sense? You talked as though you *expected* to find beings like this . . .'

The Doctor, lost in thought, nodded absently. '. . . living in a high order of civilization. And apart from that deserted, crumbling memorial, this . . . thing is the only other sign of that civilization we've seen – so far . . .'

'Are you saying you've been here before?'

'No. No, my boy – but, well – the geology of these rock

51

formations, the pools of liquid acid, and now ... this creature. They all suggest that this is the planet Vortis. It's a planet I have ... knowledge of ...'

'But you're not sure it is?'

'M'well – Vortis is in the Isop Galaxy – many light years from Earth. But according to my knowledge, it should have *no* satellites. This planet has several – see ...?'

The Doctor waved towards the pale sky where several satellites hung seemingly motionless, bathed in a faint reflected glow.

'Perhaps things have changed here ...'

'If this is Vortis,' Doctor Who muttered, 'they have changed indeed!'

Ian straightened up from staring at the dead shell and looked around again.

'Well, whatever it is, this is not getting us any nearer the ship.'

Doctor Who rose too. 'Quite, quite. Come on, my boy – we'll try this way.'

He began to retrace his steps, still glancing back at the mummified shadow on the ground.

'Not that way, Doctor – that's the way we've come.'

'Eh?' Doctor Who halted. 'Oh, er, yes – of course. Very observant of you, Chesterton.' He snapped his fingers as he now strode forward, heading up the pass. 'Well, come on, my boy!'

As Ian followed he noticed that Doctor Who's silhouette ahead of him was becoming more sharply outlined against the sky. It was getting brighter. He strode after him quickly and caught up as the pointed rocks on either side of them fell away and they emerged from the pass.

Doctor Who halted to take stock of the ground. They both peered around.

'Here, Chesterton!'

Doctor Who was pointing down. A scattering of the glassy sand over hard rock showed scratches – and the unmistakable marks of claws. They both stopped, following them clearly now, and Ian looked up to where they led.

The landscape ahead of them, featureless now except for a scatter of rock and an occasional stunted crag, rose gently upward towards a ridge.

As Ian noted it and prepared to follow the tracks, a glow swept across the sky and lit the ridge from behind so that it stood out clear and stark for a moment.

Ian halted and put out a hand to touch Doctor Who.

'Lights!' he exclaimed. 'That's no satellite!'

'Where?'

'Over there! It turned . . . swept across the sky! I'm sure it did!'

'Wait!' Doctor Who commanded.

After a moment or so, the sky glowed and the ridge lit again. It faded.

'There – don't tell me that's anything natural! It's a searchlight, or something like it, surely?'

'M'yes . . . yes. Well, we shall see when we reach the top of that ridge, I imagine.'

'The tracks lead to it – over there – and there, see?'

And Ian moved swiftly ahead, taking up the lead.

'Carefully, Chesterton. Keep your eyes open!'

But Ian was already absorbed in picking up the tracks, stumbling in his urgency up the slope, pausing only to check on the scratches and prints which the looser ground now revealed clearly in a growing radiance.

He reached the top of the ridge, paused there – and caught his breath at the sight. He remained wordless until Doctor Who, toiling painfully upward in his wake, joined him, breathing heavily.

Then Ian pointed downward, grim and questioning. Doctor Who stared at the sight beyond the ridge – at the huge glowing web-structure which lay beyond them in the shallow valley, its luminous tentacles seeming to stretch around it endlessly before they writhed and disappeared around the sentinel crags.

Above this strange, sprawling web-building a light wheeled and flashed.

'So that's where they took the ship!' Ian breathed.

53

Doctor Who rubbed his chin, narrowing his eyes as he sized up its sinister pulsating shape.

'It would seem so.' He paused uneasily. 'We'll have to go down there, of course, but . . .'

'But what? Come on!'

Doctor Who hesitated, thinking. 'I . . . wish I knew more of what we are up against . . .'

Ian halted, considered this and stared downward. He nodded, began moving carefully forward, not taking his eyes off the sight ahead of him.

'Yes' he muttered, and turned. 'Perhaps if we – Doctor, look out!'

Suddenly Ian was threshing and lashing out as, with a swish, something landed and enveloped him– a fine net, a web. He kicked and struggled in its coils.

'Go back!'

But his voice was half-drowned in a sudden humming which rose from the rocks around them, and as Doctor Who himself halted, then turned, another net swished from the shadows of a rock and enmeshed him too.

Doctor Who stood stock-still in the grip of the web-like net. He looked around.

From all directions the eyes of the Zarbi shone as they closed in on them. Their shapes appeared, sleekly bulbous, emitting their hideous chorus of chirrups that pierced the ears.

Doctor Who's mouth opened in astonishment.

'Zarbi!' he muttered.

The creatures came scuttling forward till they swarmed all around them, the pulsating light from below lighting their shapes weirdly.

Ian had fallen and lay there threshing blindly, but Doctor Who kept his feet. In the face of their terrifying appearance he strove to maintain his composure.

Calmly, with a slow gesture, Doctor Who lifted the net which enclosed him and managed to sweep it clear.

One of the Zarbi reared in front of him and its great shining eyes inspected him closely.

He stared steadily back, erect and unmoving now, at the evil shape of the creature confronting him.

Ian was shouting and writhing on the ground. He had succeeded in struggling half clear of the net but suddenly a Zarbi from the surrounding swarm lunged at him. Ian kicked out and his shoe stubbed hard against its metallic body. It checked, and Ian struggled to his feet, one arm free, wary, circling, hampered by his net, ready to kick again.

The Zarbi reared, lumbered with incredible swiftness towards him, its feelers raised. It lunged and struck with steely foreclaws.

Ian went down like a log. He stirred and still tried dazedly to get to his feet again. At that the Zarbi confronting Doctor Who emitted a shrill commanding chirrup which rose above the concerted noise, and pointed with a foreclaw.

Doctor Who's amazed stare followed the pointing foreclaw. He saw a rod-shaped instrument surrounded by a coil of glass-like tubes swivel from the nearest crag until it pointed directly down on Ian.

He froze at that, then abruptly yelled, above the din.

'Chesterton – *don't struggle!*'

Ian ceased lashing about him in his attempts to rise. He looked, dazed, in the direction in which Doctor Who was grimly pointing.

Instinctively Ian made to resist as two of the Zarbi bent their huge, evil shapes towards him.

Again Doctor Who shouted desperately.

'Don't move! If they wanted to kill us they'd have already done so! Look!'

Ian stared and saw the strange gun levelled directly at him from a crag, with the shiny head and glowing eyes of a Zarbi behind it.

'They have weapons!'

'Yes! Now do as I say! Obey them!'

A Zarbi clamped its pincer claw on Ian's arm. He winced at its grip, but submitted. Another gripped him and together the creatures dragged Ian to his feet.

'You mean – you're going to let them take us . . . down there?'

'What else? What can we do anyway? The brain you were given, Chesterton – such as it is – *use it!*'

Doctor Who turned to ponder the gun. 'Interference . . .' he muttered. '. . . the way the ship's door behaved . . . could it have come from that . . . ? A magnostatic gun . . .? I . . . wonder . . .!'

Ian was on his feet. He groped to raise the net, and now that he had ceased struggling, the Zarbi, chirruping all around him, made no move as he succeeded in tearing off the net.

But one of them kept its cruel claw clamped agonizingly tight on his arm. Ian looked about him.

'It's these things that are making that sound. Could we . . . try talking to them, do you think? Make them understand?'

Doctor Who grunted. 'I doubt it. Short of rubbing our back legs together like some sort of grasshopper. No. I'm afraid I haven't the key to this kind of grammar.'

The Zarbi confronting Doctor Who, apparently the leader of this swarm, gestured to the two men with a foreclaw in a unmistakable sign of command.

'It wants us to move on. That's clear enough anyway.' Ian stood his ground sullenly. Doctor Who shouted impatiently, 'For heaven's sake, Chesterton, at least it will lead us to the ship!'

'Even if it's the last thing we ever see!' Ian retorted, and as the Zarbi thrust him forward, he wrenched his hand wildly to be free and backed away. Immediately a fresh chorus of angry chirrups broke out and the Zarbi surrounding Ian closed in towards him.

Again Doctor Who shouted desperately, 'No, my boy! Save your energy for when we can use it!'

Ian glowered back and shrugged. He allowed himself to be led forward as his Zarbi captors pulled at his arms. He looked with loathing about him at the chirruping swarm, and muttered as Doctor Who came abreast of him, 'You were right. These crawlies are nothing like the thing we saw back there, on the ground.'

Doctor Who nodded. 'Quite. It's all much different from what I expected . . .'

'It could scarcely be worse,' Ian snarled, and grimaced at the merciless tugging on his hands.

'It's the planet Vortis, all right, just the same.'

'Did you expect this to happen too?' Ian asked bitterly, and nodded about him at the rearing, shiny shapes of the Zarbi herding them towards the strange web building.

'I didn't *choose* to land on Vortis,' the Doctor snapped. 'But yes – one would expect to find the Zarbi here.'

'Zarbi – is that what these things are called?'

Doctor Who nodded stiffly. 'But what I didn't expect was to find them . . . behaving like this . . .'

'Then how? Were *they* supposed to scuttle away at the sight of *us* – or greet us with speeches of welcome and garlands of forget-me-nots?'

'I meant,' Doctor Who said coldly, 'that I didn't expect to find them acting with any organized intelligence at all, which is rather more than *you* are showing. Hm. Yes – it's that which fascinates me . . .'

'*Fascinates* you?' Ian snorted. 'It just gives me the creeps!'

Now there was movement everywhere. The crags which dotted their descent seemed to be alive as the shapes of more Zarbi emerged from them and joined the swarm which was hustling the Doctor and Ian down the rock-littered slope.

Out of the corner of his eye Ian saw something new and even stranger. A Zarbi scuttled into sight on top of a crag. It pointed downward and waved a foreclaw in an oddly precise gesture of command.

In answer, something moved on the rock. It was a living thing, but not a Zarbi.

Ian caught at Doctor Who with his free hand pointed. They both stared.

Something else was scuttling down the rock – an animal, and as the pulsing light from the web-building in the valley shone its ray towards them it lit the creature briefly.

It was like a giant wood grub, with more legs than a

centipede beneath a rounded, scaly, armoured back – and an evil pointed snout.

'What is it?'

'A grub of sorts. But huge . . .'

'And we thought this planet was deserted! It's swarming with life! All of it horrible!'

Doctor Who was frowning, racking his mind to identify this new creature more precisely. 'Larva . . . he muttered to himself. He looked again towards the grub-like creature and saw that, each time the Zarbi on the rock gestured, it changed its direction in obedience to the sign. Ian saw it too.

'It's that Zarbi that's moving it about! Has he got it on some sort of string . . .?'

Doctor Who was looking intently. In his fascination he had halted.

'No,' he said. No . . . but you're right. It's being . . . controlled.'

An angry chirrup rose from his Zarbi captor. With a wrench of a steely foreclaw it hustled the Doctor along so that the old man stumbled and nearly fell.

He marched on, looking backward, deep in thought.

'There's another!' Ian said, pointing.

Another grub, its long sharp snout pointed directly down at them, moved faintly on a rock ledge above them. Behind it was poised the feeler of a Zarbi. The foreclaw moved faintly against the sky, and as it did so the grub turned slightly, following Ian and Doctor Who with its snout as they passed on down the slope.

Doctor Who exclaimed suddenly, 'I have it!'

'What?'

'Venom grubs! Let me see . . . – yes! That would fit. But . . .' The doctor wagged his head, puzzled.

'. . . venom? . . . you mean, those things are poisonous?'

'I mean they lived on venom . . .'

'Ugh!' Ian said. 'Charming!'

'Well, as I recollect from my studies of the Isop Galaxy, they used to serve a very useful purpose. You saw that long proboscis?'

'That snout, you mean. Wicked isn't it? I shouldn't like to get a jab from that!'

'Neither did their enemies. You see, their hard shell made them impervious to attack themselves. If a poisonous creature attacked them, it couldn't penetrate the shell. But with that snout, the venom grubs could pierce anything. They would seek out their attacker's poison sac, and impale it.

'You mean, *disembowel* them?'

'No. Puncture them. Disarm them. By – drawing out their poison.'

'Oh!' Ian stared back with rather more interest.

'But there's something which puzzles me,' Doctor Who said. He walked a few paces, submitting tamely to the hustling of his Zarbi captors.

'I'm glad I'm not the only one who's puzzled,' Ian said savagely, glaring around him.

'Well, it's this,' the Doctor said sombrely. 'The venom grubs have changed their habits too.'

'How?'

'The Zarbi were once their natural enemies. Now they appear to have ... tamed them. The question is – *how* the Zarbi tamed them ... and what for?'

'Not for household pets, I shouldn't think,' Ian said. 'Venom grubs, eh? I'd rather keep a pet cobra.'

'No,' agreed Doctor Who. 'Not for household pets.'

Now the glowing building with its writhing tentacles stretching far out over the land, loomed ahead of them with the great wheeling light at its apex. More chirruping broke out among the Zarbi as they shoved the two men towards an opening in the enormous web. The opening glowed more brightly than the mass of interlaced strands which almost covered it, and as they came closer, Ian and Doctor Who saw that the opening was in fact the mouth of a tunnel leading far inside.

They paused instinctively, awed by all this strangeness, and were shoved on into the tunnel. Ian stared around him. Even the concave walls of the tunnel were made of web, and as he looked, he saw it move, faintly but clearly. Small globules swelled at the entrance to the tunnel. The globules expanded, broke into web patterns, and stretched outward, then solidified, extending the tunnel minutely as they did so.

'Doctor – see that? That stuff is growing . . .!'

Doctor Who looked more closely. 'Mm . . . yes – so I see. Organic matter, I imagine – reproducing itself.'

'But that's fantastic!'

'It happens on your own planet, remember.'

'Among tiny forms of life, maybe,' Ian retorted. 'But not like this! This . . . building, whatever you call it, why – it's enormous! Bigger, even, than it looked from the ridge!'

'Quite. And . . . stretching out across the planet. How long has it taken to reach this size, I wonder? Mm? A hundred years? *Two* hundred? *More*?'

'But why? What for? These Zarbi creatures can obviously live outside of it. What use is a web to them? It doesn't seem built to *catch* anything, does it?'

Doctor Who sighed. 'My dear boy, I wish I could answer all your questions. Unfortunately I'm as puzzled as you are.'

Now the Zarbi began heckling them with angry, impatient chirrupings, and those nearest roughly shoved the Doctor forward again. He turned testily, but as always kept his dignity.

'Yes, all right – don't push!' Nevertheless, he stared with some misgiving inward, along the mysterious tunnel which seemed to taper to infinity. He summoned a jaunty cheerfulness.

'Well, the key to it all is undoubtedly inside . . . somewhere. Lead on, my boy.'

'Tell me what else I can do!' Ian growled. He gestured dismally ahead of them. 'Come into my parlour – said the spider to the fly.'

Doctor Who stared and pondered that quotation grimly. He braced himself and stepped forward into the tunnel.

Inside *Tardis* it was now absolutely still. Vicki remained frozen for a long time, gripping the control table, staring at the scanner screen. It was blank. She could not hear a sound.

Finally she ventured to turn.

She saw the exit doors were opened. She had not heard them. She could no longer stand the silence, the utter quiet after her turbulent, terrifying journey. She had at least to see where they now were. Cautiously she approached the door, and looked out.

She could see part of a huge webbed ceiling, the flat floor. The rest was screened by a partition wall.

As far as she could see the place was empty. Vicki took a timid step out of the ship, and halted. Only a silence answered her. She walked carefully forward, past the wall.

The police-box shape of *Tardis* stood in a huge room under a great webbed vault of a roof. A vast panel on one wall shone with strange controls. There were dials, buttons and flashing light patterns like nothing an earthly eye would recognize or understand.

Dominating these controls were two patterns.

The first was a completely circular web composed entirely of minute buttons of light. Only a portion of this web was illuminated.

Beside it was an enlarged segment of the same web – a wedge-shaped thirty-degree slice of it, similarly illuminated. Near its pointed apex a tiny cluster of lights blazed and twinkled. They were moving, converging on the pointed tip of the web segment.

Their movement was repeated on the smaller, complete web. There, a small single light inched slowly in along one segment of the web towards the centre.

Vicki halted and gaped at it. The pattern of lights, converging on the centre of the web-plan, was the only thing which moved in the entire room. It drew her, fascinated, her fear forgotten, and she walked on into the centre of the huge room.

As she did so, a sound erupted suddenly and shattered the stillness – a piercing, concerted chirruping.

She turned in horror, her hands flying to her ears – and saw the Zarbi everywhere. Several of them scuttled out from behind *Tardis* and waited there, cutting off any chance of her running back into the ship.

Other Zarbi had appeared through webbed tunnel doors leading off from this room and now converged on her. At a few paces away they halted – and only one advanced, rearing on its hind legs, its eyes glowing down upon her.

Vicki screamed. She cowered and backed – but there was no retreat, for she was surrounded by these nightmarish creatures, whose faces she had first seen through the scanner.

She saw that the Zarbi now towering over her held an odd implement in its foreclaw. It glittered. It was shaped rather like a large wishbone, and it shone like gold. The Zarbi reached forward to her and she screamed again, shrinking back until she felt her arms seized in a vice-like hold from behind.

Now she was frozen with horror. The Zarbi facing her reached down with the wishbone-shaped implement towards her face, and though she wrenched her head desperately this way and that, it snapped the open end of the wishbone around her throat, like a necklet.

With that, Vicki's struggling, her screaming, the agonizing fear she felt, all faded.

Her eyes took on a glazed expression and her face relaxed into a dullness as though she were hypnotized. Her arms dropped and she stood motionless.

Now the leading Zarbi held up its claw, pointing at her, then moved its foreleg till it pointed to the inner wall.

Slowly in exact obedience to its gesture, Vicki turned and walked dazedly to the wall. She halted and stood there, blank faced, apparently unseeing.

Now the Zarbi gave their attention to *Tardis* as their leader turned its great luminous eyes on the ship. It scuttled forward. The other Zarbi moved back to make way. At the door of the ship the Zarbi halted, and another Zarbi detached itself from the swarm in the control room to join it.

Together they peered inside. A chirrup of surprise escaped the leader. It moved forward for a closer inspection, ready to climb inside, and rested its foreclaw against the ship's hull.

As it did so, a spark crackled and flashed between the hull

and its claw. With a loud, high-pitched shriek, the Zarbi leader pitched backward, hurled from the ship's door, and collapsed sprawling on the floor, its legs waving feebly, the luminous glare in its eyes blinking and fading.

Slowly, dazed, it scrambled to its feet, and pulling at its companion, it scuttled in retreat from the ship's doors.

A high-pitched whistle came from the control wall and the Zarbi turned. The cluster of lights which had been inching forward now reached the centre of the web pattern, which flashed a bright winking light signal.

The Zarbi leader motioned and turned towards the doorway of a tunnel leading into the room.

On the threshold stood Doctor Who and Ian. Behind them in the tunnel their Zarbi escorts swarmed. Prodded forward by their captors, Ian and the Doctor stumbled, staring about them, into the control room.

Ian turned, saw the ship – then Vicki.

'Vicki!'

Vicki remained impassive, blank, unseeing. Ian strode across, ignoring the Zarbi now, and grabbed Vicki by the shoulders, staring at her.

'What's the matter? Vicki – what have they done?'

She gave no answer, staring through and past him. He shook her, then saw the wishbone-shaped necklet around her throat. He snatched at this and dropped it on the floor. As he did so, Vicki blinked. Life and awareness returned, flooding her face, and she awoke to a delighted smile.

'Ian! Oh – Ian . . .!'

She threw her arms around Ian's neck and buried her head on his chest. He patted her, murmuring, 'It's all right, Vicki – it's all right . . .'

The Zarbi had concentrated their attention on Doctor Who, propelling him against a wall. He stood there stiff and austere – and now the Zarbi leader gestured.

From one of the hatches along the outer wall a creature emerged. It was a venom grub. It waddled forward on its countless legs with incredible swiftness, entirely under the direction of the leading Zarbi's pointing claw. It turned until it was opposite Doctor Who, its long spear-shaped snout pointing directly at him.

Ian let go of Vicki and started forward, glaring. 'What do you think you're doing?'

Two Zarbi reared and snatched at him, clamping their claws tight on him . . . Ian struggled and fought, raving, but was held mercilessly firm. Other Zarbi guards grabbed Vicki. She shrieked.

Doctor Who, backed up against the wall, stared helpless and a little unnerved at the venom grub's snout which pointed implacably at him. Ian, still struggling, stared horrified.

'Doctor!' Vicki shrieked. 'What are they doing? Please – *no*!' She lapsed into terrified sobbing. Doctor Who put up a trembling hand and summoned a smile for her.

'Try not to be afraid, child,' he said gently. 'There's nothing you can do.'

The Zarbi leader gave a sudden sharp gesture with its claw. At that, a spark crackled from the snout of the venom grub. Ian flinched.

Beside the Doctor's head, the wall discoloured. It singed and then began to smoke.

Now the Zarbi directed the venom grub slowly. Its snout spat more sparks, and in obedience to the Zarbi's directions, the smoking the discoloration on the wall moved upward, then across, . . . and finally downward – until it had described a burned circle outlining the Doctor's head against the wall.

Now the Zarbi leader paused and directed the venom grub away with a final gesture. It backed and retreated.

Doctor Who expelled a long breath. He managed an ashen smile.

Vicki went limp. Ian relaxed and ceased to struggle. Doctor Who wagged his head wonderingly.

'Hmm – yes . . . I must say, I did have my doubts for a moment – but I *thought*, or, er, at least, I *hoped* it would turn out to be . . . a demonstration only.'

'What of, for goodness sake?'

'Of their power,' Doctor Who said simply. 'That's clearly what it was.'

'But why bother?' Ian protested. 'They can do anything they like with us!'

Now the Zarbi leader confronted Doctor Who menacingly. It held up its foreclaw, chirruping harshly – and pointed

towards *Tardis*. Another Zarbi gestured again to the motionless venom grub, summoning it with a foreclaw, guiding it till the great armour-backed insect had wheeled to threaten Ian and Vicki; she caught her breath, clung to Ian, and called nervously 'What do they want, Doctor?'

Ian said, frowning, 'It looks as if they want something out of the ship.'

'Yes. They don't seem keen on going inside themselves. Why, I wonder?'

The Zarbi leader gestured again, impatiently. This time it

pointed at the venom grub, at Ian and Vicki, then again directed Doctor Who towards the ship. Doctor Who sighed, inclined his head obediently.

'I must do as they say – whatever that is. Otherwise . . .' He grimaced and smiled at them, and walked towards *Tardis*.

Ian and Vicki stared after him. Ian muttered, 'Vicki – what happened after we left to explore this place?'

Vicki put a hand to her head.

'I'm . . . not sure. I was asleep. Then those noises started up, and the ship began rocking – horribly. I could see on the scanner they were dragging the ship away.'

Suddenly a thought struck Ian and he gripped Vicki by the arms.

'I completely forgot!' he said. He stared at Vicki. 'Barbara! Where is she?' He shook Vicki in a sudden fit of anxiety. '*Where's . . . Barbara?*'

In the cave from which Barbara had fled, the Menoptera now held a worried council.

Vrestin stood up and paced back and forth, his magnificent wings folded.

'I don't think the earth girl will betray us,' he declared. 'Keep watch, Challis. We others must get a warning through.'

He moved to the wall of the cave, bent down and rolled a rock aside. Challis crept towards the mouth of the cave, peered outward and took up a watchful station there.

The fourth Menoptera, Zota, caught at Vrestin's arm. He said anxiously, 'The Zarbi are all around. If we break communicator silence now, they will find us!'

Hrostar, Vrestin's deputy, shook his head.

'That we shall have to risk. Vrestin is right. We are unimportant, remember. We must get a message through.'

Vrestin was dragging a metal box out from behind the rock. Several dials shone on the face of the box, which was surmounted by an oddly shaped antenna.

He grunted. 'Hrostar . . . help me with this . . .'

'Use that and we shall be destroyed,' Zota protested fearfully.

Vrestin straightened and turned. 'If we do not contact our forces – it's *they* who face destruction.'

Vrestin switched on the box. Two small bulbs glowed into life at the ends of the antennae. A low hum sounded from the set. Vrestin turned a dial.

'We must warn them of the power we found on this planet,' he muttered. 'And the weaponry which faces them. These Zarbi are organized in a way we could never have believed – if we hadn't actually seen it . . .'

He clicked on another switch and bent towards the speaker panel in the set while Zota stared anxiously towards the cave entrance. Vrestin began calling.

'Pilot party to Menoptera invasion force. Calling Menoptera spearhead.'

He flicked up a switch while he and Hrostar listened anxiously. Static speckled their reception, crackling harshly over the speaker, but otherwise there was no response.

Vrestin frowned, flipped back the speaker switch, and repeated, 'Pilot party to Menoptera invasion force. Urgent reconnaissance report. Acknowledge please.'

They listened again. Hrostar shook his head doubtfully.

'They are within reach of the enemy locators. They will not risk breaking communicator silence.'

'They will,' Vrestin declared. 'They can bounce their signals to us off satellite Taron to mask their source.' He repeated urgently into the speaker, 'Menoptera spearhead! Acknowledge reception!'

But only the familiar crackle of static answered them. Hrostar got up.

'It's no use. The cave is blanking off our transmission.'

Vrestin rose too. 'Yes,' he muttered grimly. 'We must send from the open.'

They stared at each other, realizing what that meant. Operating a transmitter out in the open would invite certain discovery by the Zarbi. Vrestin looked towards the figures of Challis and Zota and wagged his head doubtfully over them.

'We can only hope to get a message through before . . .'

68

Vrestin did not finish the sentence. From the cave mouth came a sudden yell from Challis.

'Vrestin! Hrostar – the Zarbi . . .!'

Barbara stood at the entrance. A strange wishbone-shaped necklet encircled her throat. Her face was glazed and trance-like. On either side of her crowded the hated Zarbi, staring inward.

Vrestin lunged for the transmitter and hurled it against the cave wall with a mighty sweep, smashing it. Zota and Challis were backing before the advancing Zarbi, who pointed, directing the dazed Barbara ahead of them like a shield. Challis darted and picked up a rock. He poised this to hurl it among the Zarbi crowding forward. One of the Zarbi gestured with its claw.

A venom grub leaped forward with startling swiftness from between them. Its evil snout spat fire. Challis gave a high scream. The rock dropped from his hand and he reeled, clutching at his chest.

He collapsed to the cave floor and rolled there, twitching feebly. Smoke began to issue from his body.

Zota wheeled and shouted, 'Captain Vrestin – run! Get away!'

Vrestin, farther back in the cave, hesitated. There was nothing else for it. He turned and darted away, halted, spotting a side tunnel, charged towards it as the venom grub fired again. At that, Zota lunged for the venom grub with a raised spar – but the fire caught him. He whirled and fell, smoke rose from his face and body, and suddenly he was still.

Barbara stared unseeingly at all this as though frozen into a statue.

Wisely now, Hrostar stood stock still. A Zarbi pointed at him. Its claw signed for him to join Barbara. He bowed his head and obeyed.

Several of the Zarbi moved forward, their claws making a scuttling noise on the floor of the cave as they headed for the smashed communicator and clustered around to examine its remains.

Hrostar looked at Barbara. He saw the necklet around her

69

throat. With an eye on the Zarbi he reached and pulled it off. For a moment, while he held it, his own eyes dulled and he stood motionless. Then the necklet dropped from his nerveless fingers. He recovered.

Barbara was blinking as if awakening from a deep sleep. She cowered suddenly at the sight of the Zarbi all around them in the cave. She felt Hrostar's hand on her arm. He was sizing up the Zarbi, and said slowly, 'I think we are safe . . . for the present . . .'

'How did I get back here?'

Hrostar pointed down at the necklet he had dropped to the floor. 'You were morphatized.'

She stared at the necklet, following his pointing finger. 'I don't . . . understand . . .'

'The Zarbi can control anyone – even us, the Menoptera – who wear that metal.'

Barbara looked down at the necklet and her curiosity overcame her fear. She stooped furtively and reached out to examine it.

'It's gold . . .' she murmured.

'Don't touch it!' Hrostar said hastily.

She withdrew her hand as if stung, and touched her wrist, remembering, wondering.

'So my . . . bracelet . . .' Barbara murmured. She got up, looked around. 'Why don't they put it back? Why don't they put one on you?'

'If they want us in a trance, they will.'

Barbara gave a gasp as she saw the bodies of Zota and Challis lying motionless on the ground. Hrostar moved to shield her from the sight.

'They are . . . at peace,' he said gently.

An angry chirruping had arisen around them from the Zarbi as their leader brought back the smashed communicator box. Now they crowded threateningly about Barbara and Hrostar, prodding them towards the cave mouth with their claws.

Barbara reached fearfully to cling to Hrostar's arm. 'Where will they take us?' she whispered.

'To the Crater of Needles, most probably.'

'. . . and . . . then?'

Hrostar squared his shoulders, showing a glimpse of his beautiful wings. 'Work,' he said shortly. He turned for a brief farewell glance towards his fallen comrades, then looked grimly at Barbara.

He said, 'Once there . . . you may well wish . . . they had not spared you . . .'

In the control room of the weird Zarbi Headquarters, Ian gripped Vicki's arm reassuringly and watched Doctor Who wave his hands and attempt sign language with the Zarbi leader. The old man kept shaking his head while the Zarbi gestured impatiently towards the ship *Tardis*. Ian was puzzled.

'It beats me why the Zarbi won't go into the ship!' he muttered.

Vicki pressed her temples. 'They dare not,' she said, and looked surprised at having said that. Ian turned to look at her.

'Why not?'

Vicki waved her hand helplessly, trying to remember.

'It was . . . rather like a dream. But I seem to remember that they tried. There was a flash. The two Zarbi were . . . knocked backward. Or . . . did I just dream that . . .?'

Ian was looking at her intently. 'But – *Tardis* has no defences! If what you say is true – they must have been repelled by something . . . of their own making . . .'

Ian broke off his guessing as a flashing from the control panel on the wall caught his eye. The Zarbi now remaining in the control room saw it too and stiffened attentively, their cruel heads turning towards the web-map on the wall – where a cluster of lights on its outer perimeter glowed suddenly on and off. A speaker beneath the web-map issued a series of 'pip' sounds in time with their flashing.

'Sounds like some sort of alert,' Ian said, eyeing the alerted Zarbi.

'Yes – radar of a kind. It's not unlike the system we had on the Dido spaceship, 'Vicki said.

71

'But – these venom grubs! The Zarbi use them as weapons! That means there must be other forms of life here, or they wouldn't need them. Do they use these creatures to prey on others, or . . .'

Vicki finished the question Ian was asking himself. '– or to protect themselves?' she said.

Immediately following the flashing lights and the 'pip' warnings, a loud burst of humming and chirruping broke out from the main speaker on the control wall. A huge light above it glared on.

The Zarbi reacted to that as to a command. They moved swiftly to surround Doctor Who – and propelled him roughly, urgently, towards the centre of the room. He resisted their violent handling, roaring, 'Take your wretched claws off me, d'you hear? This minute!'

But the Zarbi ringed the Doctor and herded him into the centre of the room. There they held him. Doctor Who stared indignantly around him, ruffled and furious, until a sound from above made him look up, startled.

'Bless my soul!'

A deep, saucer-shaped dome was descending towards him from the roof. Anxiously the Doctor tried to back away, but the Zarbi held him immovable. The huge Dome came lower, slowly now, until it closed over his head. It was transparent, but through it Doctor Who's head and features were oddly distorted as though he stood in a fairground hall of mirrors.

The Doctor started and turned wonderingly as, seemingly out of nowhere, an alien voice boomed hollowly around him, inside the spiral of the Dome. The vowel sounds were distorted and echoing, and though the words were understandable, they did not issue from anything like a human throat.

The Voice boomed, 'Very well – speak-eak! . . . Why have you come to this planet-et . . .?'

Doctor Who recovered from his surprise. He turned his head this way and that, mustered a defiance, and snapped back.

'W-who are you? We come in peace . . .!'

'Peace?' the Voice echoed back at him. 'Is that why you

attack-ack? We require to know where your main force is-is . . .!'

Ian and Vicki, held at bay by the Zarbi and under the menace of a venom grub which remained pointing implacably at them, could see Doctor's Who's head, grotesquely distorted through the glassy side of the Dome, but they could hear nothing. They saw the Doctor's head turn their way. The distortion magnified his lips into a huge rubbery duck's bill.

Vicki exclaimed, 'He's speaking – to something! Why can't we hear what he's saying?'

Ian was shaking his head, bewildered. He didn't answer because he had no answer. He remained staring at the strange Dome.

Inside it Doctor Who was answering vehemently, 'I repeat – we are alone! We have strayed from our astral path!'

The Voice boomed angrily back. 'You heard the alarm. Your force is on its way-ay . . .! We wish to know when this invasion fleet will arrive, *and* its weaponry-y . . .!'

'I have *told* you – we are peaceful travellers from Earth!'

'You lie!' the Voice thundered. 'You are the Menoptera-a . . .! Our detectors show you massing in space to attack. This is your final chance to speak-eak . . .!'

A pause. Doctor Who stared. He said quietly, 'We know nothing of this . . . Menoptera force you speak of . . .'

The Voice rose to a terrifying pitch as it boomed back, raging.

'Very well-ell! We shall show you the fate that awaits *all* your ships, *all* your people-le . . .!'

The control panel on the wall beyond the Dome came to life. A series of lights flashed and a loud humming burst from the big speaker beneath them.

At that an urgent chirruping broke out among the Zarbi. Their leader wheeled, pointed at the venom grub whose snout covered Ian and Vicki.

The grub moved, turned, and slithered swiftly – towards *Tardis*.

The Zarbi gestured. The grub lifted its evil snout, pointing it directly at the ship's doors.

Even through the distorting glass of the Dome covering his head, Doctor Who saw it. He lifted his head and shouted upward.

'Listen to me! You *must* listen! I have not finished explaining . . .!'

Vicki caught at Ian's arm. She screamed.

'Ian! They are going to destroy the ship!'

Ian, staring, wrested himself free of the Zarbi who gripped his arms.

'If they do, they might as well destroy us too!'

The Zarbi controlling the venom grub raised its foreclaw, and poised it to give the signal to fire.

CHAPTER THREE

Escape to Danger

The Dome encircling Doctor Who's head rose suddenly and slid upward. The Doctor turned and saw more clearly what was about to happen to the ship. He saw Ian lunging desperately forward to prevent it.

'Chesterton, get back! Back!'

Ian checked and suddenly pressed back against the wall with Vicki. The Doctor backed too.

The Zarbi flashed down its foreclaw, and the venom grub spat a streak of flame towards the ship's hull.

They waited, horrified, expecting to see *Tardis* smoulder and burst into flame.

Instead, the venom grub kicked backwards suddenly, and overturned on its scaly armoured back. Its multiple legs threshed feebly, and as it did so, the Zarbi commanding it folded and collapsed slowly to the floor, its luminous eyes paling, its legs jerking convulsively.

Several Zarbi near their leader fell.

'The venom-gun!' Ian yelled. 'It misfired – kicked back!'

'Yes. Yes!' Doctor Who was alight with excitement. He turned, fixing a triumphant stare on Ian and Vicki.

'Remember when we were aboard that Dalek saucer? Mm? The repellent magnets?'

'Is . . . that what's happened?'

'Something of the sort,' Doctor Who snapped. 'Yes!'

Vicki was looking on fascinated at the Zarbi leader, still lying prone and threshing its steely limbs feebly.

'Look . . . look at the one who fired the gun!'

The other Zarbi near the venom grub had raised themselves, chirruping agitatedly, and now bent to help their leader upright. It recovered, reared up, its head waving groggily this way and that. A fresh, furious burst of humming came from the control panel. The Zarbi turned towards it, braced themselves visibly, and several of their number wheeled to advance on Doctor Who and his companions.

One of them had taken up several of the strange wishbone-shaped gold necklets and now held these pointed towards them. Vicki cringed back.

'Doctor – don't let them put those things on us!'

Doctor Who, trapped, looked around him as if searching for some means of escape, or of stalling the Zarbi. He looked up

at the Dome and strode to stand beneath it. The Zarbi jailer came straight for Ian and Vicki. Before it reached them Ian acted. He kicked out at the guards closing on either side of him and hurled himself at the jailer holding a necklet poised at Vicki's neck, ready to clamp it around her throat.

The Zarbi jailer lurched sideways, but immediately two of its companions were on Ian, gripping him fiercely, swaying this way and that with him as he wrestled violently to shield Vicki.

The jailer recovered his balance and moved inexorably forward to the shrinking Vicki. She moaned, twisting her head to avoid it, but the necklet closed around her neck.

Immediately she stilled her struggling. Her face grew blank. Her eyes dulled. She slumped back against the wall.

Doctor Who saw it, and saw the Zarbi turned to close now on him, too. He lifted his head and yelled desperately up towards the dome.

'Fool! Silencing us will achieve nothing! *Nothing*! It is more important that you know of the great secrets we have inside our ship!' He waved towards *Tardis*. 'You and your creatures dare not go inside! You *cannot*! Only *we* can tell you what it holds!'

Suddenly he choked, cut short, as a Zarbi, chirruping angrily, thrust a gold clamp around his neck. The Doctor staggered, stiffened.

Only Ian remained free, kicking like a madman. He lunged and sent one of his captors sprawling, then leaped to the Doctor's side. He reached and snatched the necklet from Doctor Who's neck, pulling it free.

But as Ian did so, he began to sway. He looked down dazedly, stupidly at the necklet he held, tried to drop it – but slumped and fell to the floor, his hand still clutching it.

Doctor Who revived in time to see the Zarbi restore the stricken venom grub to its feet. At a gesture from one of them it now turned to cover Doctor Who and his party – Vicki, slumped weakly against a wall, Ian lying feebly on the floor, his hand still holding a necklet – and himself.

The Zarbi 'gunner' raised a claw. At the same time its companion thrust a necklet towards Doctor Who.

'Doctor – they're going to shoot – at us!'

Doctor Who stood stiffly, helpless, waiting now for the 'fire' signal from the Zarbi. But its claw remained poised, and suddenly its eye was caught by a large light flashing from the control panel. The master light above the web indicators was

77

glowing furiously off and on. The Zarbi manning the panel roused themselves, humming and chirruping excitedly.

At the same time the great Dome in the roof again began to descend. Doctor Who's Zarbi guard lowered the trancenecklet, and instead pushed him towards the centre of the room, urging him towards the lowering dome. Doctor Who shook his head, glaring back, and put up a hand. In deliberate defiance of the Zarbi he first took a pace towards Ian and Vicki, wrenched off their necklets and cast them hurriedly, with a gesture of contempt, at the Zarbi's feet.

Ian came to himself dazedly, saw the venom grub with its vicious snout now harmlessly lowered, and noted the hum of activity around the glowing control panel.

'Lucky they changed their minds!' he muttered.

'They didn't!' Doctor Who snapped. 'These creatures have no mind to change! Something changed it for them.'

The Doctor nodded towards the descending Dome, and only now, at a further angry shove from his Zarbi guards, allowed himself to be hustled beneath it. The Dome closed down over his head.

Immediately the Voice within it boomed around him.

'If your ship is proof against our weapons – remember, you are not-ot! Tell us the secret of your armour-our . . .!'

'Impossible!' The Doctor rapped back. 'Who can tell why it withstood the fire of your . . . your gun creature, unless you tell me how *it* operates?'

The anger of the Voice which roared back around him dizzied the Doctor. 'You have the insolence to demand our secrets -- instead of yielding up your own!'

Doctor Who braced himself and thundered back.

'Then do not ask me questions I cannot answer!'

On a plateau above the cave a faint movement showed. Two waving feelers showed against the sky. Then the Menoptera Vrestin hauled himself into sight through a crevice in the ground.

He stared around him for a sign of the Zarbi party which had invaded the cave with a venom grub, killed his two comrades, and borne Hrostar and the earth girl Barbara away.

Vrestin listened. He could hear nothing. As he turned he saw a glow sweep across the ridge to his right. Staring cautiously about him he crouched low and ran dodging for the ridge. He threw himself flat upon it and peered down the other side.

He stared at the great sprawling web which spread out its glowing tentacles in the shallow valley. Cautiously Vrestin rose and began stepping warily towards it when he was suddenly alerted by a humming, coupled with a chirruping.

Immediately Vrestin dodged for the shadow of a crag and dived for cover there, watching. The shadows of two Zarbi appeared from behind him and marched past, heading down towards the great headquarters.

After a moment Vrestin rose cautiously from hiding and looked after the moving figures of the Zarbi. Looking all around him for signs of any other movement, he began shadowing them, flitting from crag to crag and making use of whatever cover the ground offered.

As the great writhing shape of the web building appeared before him he turned, noting how its tentacles curled around rocks and crags, the globular tips puffing, bursting and throwing out fresh web patterns as they inched forward over the land. Vrestin halted uncertainly. Beyond him the two Zarbi stood at a recess in the tangled mass of web.

As he watched, a section of webbing rose before them like a portcullis, revealing a tunnel-like corridor beyond, leading inward. The Zarbi moved in, and the entrance slid down behind them with a whirring sound, blotting them from his view.

Carefully Vrestin began to circle the great structure, looking intently around him.

Inside the Dome Doctor Who was still shouting back defiantly at the Voice while Vicki and Ian watched and wondered. They could hear nothing, and could see only his face, which distorted with every movement through the Dome as he answered his inquisitor. His arms waved and gestured angrily.

The Voice had changed its tone from thunderous anger to a booming menace.

'You speak of the great secrets in your ship. You will give them to us to use against the invader. In return you will be given ...' the Voice paused ... '... your ... freedom ...'

Doctor Who hesitated. 'What of the fourth member of our party? Where is she?'

A silence answered him.

'Well?'

'She has been taken to the Crater of Needles-les. She will be restored to you – *after* you have helped us ... Now – will your secrets look into the stars?'

The question puzzled the Doctor. He called back, 'I, er, have an astral map, if that is what you mean ...'

'Will it show where the Menoptera are massing-ing ...? Where they will ... land-and ...?

'You say it is the Menoptera who are invading this planet?'

The answer was partly lost in echoing sounds. Doctor Who cupped a hand to his ear to shield it against the reverberations.

'... somewhere in space ... beyond the range of our locators ... they are grouping ... scattering false trails to mislead us ... their numbers are great-eat ... I am aware only of movement ... ent ...'

'You – cannot determine their position?'

'This is what I require you to do-o ...'

Doctor Who paused as though considering that. He decided on a bluff, but his voice as he answered was innocent. 'I shall ... need assistance.'

'Bring your ... astral map out of your ship.' The Voice boomed back.

'Even to do that, I shall need help ...'

Doctor Who waited for the answer, hopefully. His face took on a dismayed expression as no answer came. Instead the Dome rose from his head into the air towards the roof. He looked anxiously towards Ian and Vicki, and muttered anxiously to himself, 'What will it do now?'

His answer came in the form of a sudden hum of instructions from the speaker on the control panel. The Zarbi there stiffened attentively to its stream of intermittent humming, chirruping. Doctor Who moved towards Ian and Vicki. One Zarbi remained covering them, the venom grub hovering on the floor with its snout aimed in their direction.

The Zarbi leader moved from the control panel towards the ship *Tardis*. At the same time it signalled orders to a group of Zarbi, who turned on Doctor Who and Ian and propelled them, too, towards the ship.

The Zarbi leader was at the ship's doors when suddenly it halted, drew back its foreclaws hastily, as if remembering. It motioned Ian and the Doctor to go in.

The Doctor went in first. Ian followed, looking back at the Zarbi – and beyond them to a frightened Vicki, now alone under the obscene menace of the venom grub and its guard.

'They're keeping well away from the ship,' Ian muttered.

'Yes – they've learned their lesson, my boy.'

Ian looked around as Doctor Who moved towards one of the control table sections. He flicked a lever, pulled, and the table came out easily on its smooth rollers. Ian stared in dismay.

'You really are going to dismantle the ship – for *them*?'

'Of course not, my boy. Just the astral map. Now come around this side and give it a push!'

Ian shrugged. 'I never thought I'd see you give in this easily,' he said coldly.

Doctor Who stared. '*I – give in*?'

'You don't mean you really believe they'll free us if we help?'

'Chesterton, we've made a bargain!'

'With *those* weirdies?' Ian waved with incredulous contempt to the control room beyond the ship's doors.

'Personally, I don't blame those "weirdies" as you call them for mistrusting us,' Doctor Who retorted, 'they're being invaded! Their very existence is at stake!'

Ian halted. 'Look, we might have landed in the middle of a space war, but it has nothing to do with us!'

Suddenly the Doctor was smiling at him with a hint of mischief. 'Did you really think I'd let them use me like that – unless I had something of my own in mind? Really, my boy . . .!'

Ian stared suspiciously. 'What are you up to? What are you planning?'

'Now, now – help me get this equipment moving. We don't want to leave Vicki out there on her own too long . . .'

Ian scowled and obeyed, pulling out several plug-leads which joined this section of the control table to the ship's wall. To his surprise, Doctor Who turned and demanded.

'Who told you to un-plug those leads?'

'Bit old-fashioned, isn't it, Doctor? Leads – in *Tardis*?'

'It is not common or garden flex, Chesterton! This is *Tardis* machinery. It needs a time-space link. Now plug them back!'

Ian shrugged, complied, then helped the Doctor shove the control table towards the door.

The Zarbi waiting beyond in the control room drew back as they emerged, propelling the control section containing the astral map. Ian stumbled over the leads which kept it connected to *Tardis*' machinery.

The Zarbi guard allowed Vicki past him as she moved to join them. Doctor Who put a comforting arm around her, patted her, smiled.

The other Zarbi clustered curiously around the control table as the two men wheeled and shoved it towards the centre of the great room. As it came to a halt, Doctor Who moved to the table, lifted a lid, revealing a complex panel of cathode tubes and instrument dials. He began to turn switches, scanning the astral map. Vicki stared from the Doctor to Ian.

'Are we really going to help them?' she whispered.

Ian gave a faint shake of his head. 'He's up to something crafty,' he said darkly. 'But don't ask me what.'

Doctor Who kept watching the astral map, turning dials and flipping buttons on the control panel. Suddenly he threw up his hands in impatient disgust.

'Useless — useless . . .!' he stormed. He strode suddenly across the room until he stood beneath the Dome, and there raised his hand above his head and clicked his fingers imperiously.

'Come on, come on!' he snapped. 'Put me through . . .!'

In answer, the Dome lowered down towards him. The Voice boomed expectantly, 'You have the information — already?'

'Good gracious no! No — some power source of yours has jammed my instruments! While it operates I cannot possibly use them!'

The Voice rose to an echoing bellow of anger.

'Do not dictate terms-erms . . . This is trickery-y!'

'Is it?' Doctor Who thundered back into the glassy head-piece. 'You know our ship cannot take off because of your power interference! It is that which is crippling my instruments!'

A pause ensued. For a moment Doctor Who expected the Dome to raise and end their exchange. Finally the Voice echoed back.

'I cannot suspend my functions for your experiments!'

'Very well! That's the end of it! Then get this hair-drier thing off my head! Since we cannot help you locate these invaders, you must do as you will with us!' And the Doctor thumped his fist angrily against the inner wall of the Dome. As soon as the Dome had risen sufficiently he came storming towards Ian and Vicki, throwing up his hands in a gesture of resignation.

'I've told them they can do what they like with us! I'll not lend my help to any creature which doesn't understand reason!'

And the Doctor lined himself up against the wall with Ian and Vicki and folded his arms. Ian pointed at the Zarbi, several of whom now turned menacingly towards them.

'Aren't you carrying your little game of bluff a bit far. They'll *kill* us!

Doctor Who smiled faintly. 'Will they ?' he said. He turned and waved airily towards the control panel. The Zarbi manning it were a-quiver with attentiveness as the master-light dominating it began to blaze forth. Vicki turned an astounded look to Doctor Who.

'What did you do?'

Doctor Who shrugged, faintly pleased with himself. 'I asked them to turn off their power. Told them there was interference . . .'

'Is there?' Ian asked.

'Some . . . some,' the Doctor admitted. He smiled again. 'But not as much as I made them think. Ah, here we go again!'

The Dome was coming down. Doctor Who strode through the now-bustling Zarbi and stood, waiting. The Voice began as soon as the Dome covered the doctor's ears.

'I will close down certain machinery in the vicinity of your instruments! If you try to take advantage of this – you will all die!'

Before Doctor Who could reply the Dome vanished again skyward, towards the ceiling. He looked around.

Abruptly, the web indicator lights on the control panel blanked out.

Then the large-scale segment of web, its wedge-shaped outline ablaze with tiny light buttons, faded and went dead.

The dials on the control room wall ebbed slowly down to zero. As they did so Ian stared in surprise at the effect of all this on their Zarbi guards. One of the Zarbi at the control panel slumped lazily forward and leaned its upper quarters tiredly against the controls. The luminous glare of its eyes faded and blanked out, too.

Doctor Who was too busy to pay attention to these strange happenings.

At the turn of a switch his astral map came alive. Planets and satellites winked clearly into sight on its glowing grid around the large central shape of the planet on which they had landed. Doctor Who stared intently, measuring off distances on the grid and muttering excitedly to himself.

'It is . . . yes, it *is* – the planet Vortis! And the satellites – they *must* be new! They *must* be . . .!

He continued to manipulate switches and to measure, calculate. Ian turned to look at the Zarbi nearest them. Two of these had slumped to the floor. Their glaring eyes had dimmed and their legs waved feebly, idly tracing patterns on the floor. They appeared to have lost all interest in the proceedings. Another Zarbi lurched tiredly across the floor to join his companions, slumped and dazed at the control table.

'Doctor – look . . . over there . . .!

But Doctor Who was too intent on his astral map. He worked feverishly, turning new switches and orientating the astral map to light up new quarters in the skies around this planet, Vortis.

Suddenly he exclaimed, 'Ah!'

'But doctor, the Zarbi . . .!'

Doctor Who ignored him. Staring at the astral map, he said triumphantly, 'They've good reason to believe their planet is being invaded! It *is*, my boy! It *is*! Look!'

Ian joined him. Doctor Who was pointing at the large circular blob in the centre of the astral map.

'Vortis,' he said. Then his finger moved to where a cluster of faint pinpoints blinked faintly. 'Watch there!' he muttered.

The pinpoints were moving, very slowly – towards Vortis.

'What is it – an advance wave?'

Doctor Who nodded. 'Almost certainly!'

Ian stared for a moment, until a movement from Vicki made him turn, alarmed. Vicki had crossed cautiously to where one of the Zarbi lay almost motionless. She was reaching out her hand to take up one of the gold wishbone necklets. He leaped towards her.

'Vicki – don't touch them!'

It was too late. Vicki was holding up the gold slave necklet and showing it to him. She smiled delightedly.

'It's all right! They don't work any more! See! Doctor . . .!

Doctor Who looked briefly, nodded. 'Quite so, child. This whole section is immoblized, you see. Look at their controls. All lights out. All indicators at zero.'

'No power!' Ian said. 'Nothing to interfere with the ship! We could take off, couldn't we?'

Doctor Who inclined his head. 'I daresay we could – if we wished. But . . . do we?'

Ian considered that. His face fell. 'I forgot,' he mumbled. 'No. We can't. Not without . . . Barbara.'

'Quite.'

Ian looked at the immobile Zarbi. 'But look – if *I* was to get out of here, while all these Zarbi are half-asleep . . .'

Doctor Who gripped Ian's arm and turned to point him towards the control panel. 'Chesterton, only in here are those creatures powerless! Outside this room they will be watching, waiting . . .!'

'Just the same,' Ian persisted stubbornly,' . . . if I could get to Barbara in that . . . Crater of Needles you spoke of . . . if we were all together, then we *could* get away – if this situation . . .' he waved at the powerless Zarbi . . . 'if this were repeated . . .'

'My dear fellow, you don't even know where the Crater of Needles is!'

'I'll find it,' Ian said, looking around the walls, calculating the exits. He began to move away purposefully.

'Chesterton – use your head! Come back!'

Ian paused. He shook his head. With his foot he stirred a recumbent Zarbi. It rolled a little, but raised no objection.

'See? It's no good, Doctor. I've already decided. If I'm caught, we can hardly be worse off than we are already . . .'

Doctor Who gave a resigned sigh, wagged his head half in agreement.

Ian smiled at them. Then he turned and stepped carefully to an open web door covering the tunnel through which they had come into this place.

'Ian—!' Vicki cried, and moved to stop him.

Ian paused, looked down the tunnel and suddenly darted down into it, vanishing from their sight. The Zarbi, some of them stirring feebly, made no real move to stop him. One looked blankly towards the tunnel and then turned its head disinterestedly away.

Vicki turned her anxious face to Doctor Who. His face was grave. He patted Vicki's head.

'Don't worry child – he'll be back. He may not have *my* brain, but he's fairly good at looking after himself . . .'

The Doctor masked his own uneasiness, and managed to give her a hopeful smile. Then the Doctor turned again to his instruments, flipping the controls to take a fresh view of space on the astral map. During this his receiver–transmitter, its On switch glowing and giving off only a faint, whistling whine, abruptly gave forth static as he rotated a frequency control and the curious hollow echoes that accompanied a station in operation made him halt. A whisper sounded on the radio. He listened, tense, expectant, and adjusted the volume control, the tuner. The whisper was blurred by static.

'. . . advance units . . .' it droned softly.

Suddenly the radio boomed louder, crackling, and the voice over the radio sounded high and harsh.

'. . . will rendezvous . . .'

It faded again. Vicki was staring. 'Is . . . that the Menoptera . . . speaking . . .?'

Doctor Who turned the volume control higher, gripped the tuner delicately, listened hard. He nodded.

A voice crackled over the radio speaker, coming in loudly now.

'Menop pathfinder to Leader One . . . Range to Vortis one-four-owe leagues . . .'

Doctor Who turned abruptly to Vicki. 'The recorder, Vicki, switch it on!'

Vicki hurried to obey the Doctor's pointing finger. She pressed a recorder and together they bent to the speaker, listening hard.

Now a new voice came on the airwaves, louder, more powerful, heavily speckled with static.

'Leader to spearhead. Lock course on bearing two-six-five. Speed point owe-one of light. We jettison craft at altitude two-five leagues. Individual descent . . . to group on Sayo plateau at north end of Crater of Needles . . .'

The voice faded, and with it the static, as a click sounded and the transmitter closed, leaving only a light whisper of

sound, an emptiness. Doctor Who turned to Vicki, pointed to
their small recorder.

'Did you get it?'

Vicki nodded. She was staring. 'They're going to land
near the Crater of Needles . . . ? where you said Barbara is . . .
The place Ian is trying to find . . .'

She stared towards the tunnel where Ian had disappeared.

Ian, treading carefully, had come quite a long way down the
narrow, empty tunnel. As he looked around him he saw that,
at long intervals, webbed gates were set in the wall, opening
into other passages leading off the tunnel.

He paused. A throbbing sound was coming to him from
somewhere, mingled with a faint chirruping.

Ahead of him and to his right, he saw a wide gap in the
tunnel where another bigger tunnel crossed it. He rounded it
carefully and came into an immense corridor. He had only
taken a couple of paces along this before he halted, stared
about at a new sound, and swiftly ducked into a recess –
another small tunnel.

The chirruping grew swiftly louder. As Ian flattened himself against the wall of the recess, two Zarbi appeared around
a bend in the main corridor and scuttled on past him.

He waited, wiping his face in his sleeve. Then he stepped
into the main corridor, peered up and down. It appeared
empty. He stepped out and headed down it, away from the
direction the Zarbi had taken.

He estimated that if he continued in the same general
direction, it would take him away from the control room in
the Zarbi Headquarters and perhaps, finally, to the outside
of this huge, rambling complex of webs laced with tunnels.

But it was clearly too dangerous to keep to the main corridor. Better to slip off into a side tunnel and to see if he could
zig-zag through this maze while keeping roughly parallel to
it. After all – he reasoned – if this place was constructed like
a web, then its tunnels would probably lead outward from
the centre. *If* he had taken the correct direction . . .

He dodged down a side tunnel and went warily along it,

seeking a further turning along it to correct his direction. Distantly he could still hear the humming which betrayed the presence of Zarbi activity.

He saw that this corridor ended in a webbed gate. Suddenly Ian heard a loud chirruping, so close that it pierced his ears. A Zarbi guard had reared up at the door, its back turned to him.

Ian pressed himself against the wall. He peered to see if the Zarbi was alone. It was. It had relaxed and was now crouched by the door.

What was it guarding? A gate, leading outward? What else could it be?

Ian sidled along the wall towards the unaware Zarbi. He was almost on the creature when it turned and saw him. It reared up, chirruping loudly, and Ian leaped desperately forward.

But the Zarbi was astonishingly quick. Its foreleg lashed and its cruel pincer closed on Ian's throat. He choked and threshed, trying desperately to prise open the claw, the hideous humming around his ears now deafening him.

He kicked – and the pincer relaxed its hold. Again Ian kicked – and scrambled free. He poised, and aimed a rabbit punch at the joint between the evil head and shiny body – the tiny, thin neck.

The Zarbi guard sagged. Ian hit again, at the same spot, and it dropped like a stone, still, its feelers stiff, the lights of its eyes dimmed. Gasping, feeling his throat, Ian moved on into the wider space before the webbed door. He examined it. There seemed no way of opening it.

He touched it.

Immediately a hooter shriek shattered the stillness all around him. Ian jumped and wheeled, alarmed. Then with the warning howl of the hooter echoing down the empty corridor he shook the door desperately in an attempt to force it. The sweat streamed down his face as he tore at the door.

There was nothing for it – he would have to get out of this corridor. He turned to run back from the door, but as he did so another webbed door swished down in front of him, walling him in completely as he ran into it. He smashed his fist against it in despair – and this set off another siren howl, higher pitched but just as loud.

Now the Zarbi guard trapped with him between these two doors was coming round. No matter how Ian pulled, the webbed door gave but would not open, nor break.

Now he heard an ominous humming-and-chirruping, approaching. He could hear it even above the warning hooters. At his feet the Zarbi guard was now weakly trying to rise.

Ian sprang past the Zarbi to wrest again at the outer door. As he did so a venom grub appeared in the corridor, and behind it a swarm of Zarbi guards. He heard their chirruping and turned as the grub rushed swiftly down towards him. Outside the webbed trap which now caged Ian in, it paused. Its Zarbi controller halted, raised a foreclaw. Ian hurled himself to the side of the cell formed by the two webbed gates. The venom grub spat fire.

The webbed outer door crackled, flashed, and a column of acrid smoke billowed up as the grubs' blast tore a great hole in it, revealing the open landscape of Vortis beyond it.

Ian scrambled to his feet and clawed his way through the burning hole. He staggered out and ran blindly on. Dimly ahead of him he saw a crag which reared out of the sparse landscape. He raced for its shelter while behind him he heard the massed chirruping and the humming of the Zarbi swarming at the gate.

He paused at the crag, looked back, then around him, and ran on.

Suddenly the control room blazed into life. The web maps glared, their shapes outlined in glittering buttons of light. The big central light pulsed. A humming broke from the speaker.

Doctor Who and Vicki looked up, startled, from their astral map. The Zarbi had sprung to life, too – and a venom gun controller among them turned and was suddenly menacing the Doctor and Vicki with the squat malignant shape of a sting grub, its master's claw poised ready to fire it.

Beyond the control room a further humming and chirruping echoed inward from distant tunnels, together with the wailing of warning hooters.

'Already?' Doctor Who muttered. 'It can't be! Yet it sounds as if we're under attack!'

Vicki caught at his arm despairingly. 'It's Ian – I know it is! They've found him!'

A Zarbi was now pointing at Doctor Who, and indicating the Dome. It slid down towards the Doctor from the ceiling. He stepped obediently beneath it, and the tirade which greeted him nearly knocked him over.

'You were warned!' the Voice thundered. 'Your request was a trick – to cover the escape!'

Doctor Who drew himself up. 'Nonsense, *nonsense!*' he snapped back. 'We are not responsible for that young man's behaviour!'

'You plotted with him-im . . .!'

'Really? If it was a plan – then why did I not go with him too? Eh?'

At that the tirade halted. Then . . .

'You will no longer be trusted.'

'Were we ever?' Doctor Who answered coldly. He sighed. 'Very well. Then I take it that the information I have gathered is of no use to you . . .'

The Voice interrupted him. 'Information? Of the Menoptera invasion?'

'What did you think I was talking about – the weather?' Doctor Who roared back irritably.

'Speak!' the Voice commanded.

Doctor Who hesitated. 'I'm . . . still collating my instrument readings . . .'

'– you lie! It is another of your tricks!'

'That is for you to decide. *Am* I lying? Or do I *really* have something of importance for you? Think, before you make up your mind!'

The Doctor clamped his mouth shut, expecting another outburst all around him in the echoing Dome.

Instead, abruptly, it lifted, and he was free of it. Vicki moved to the Doctor's side. He was looking upward with a faint, pleased smile. He turned. A signal hummed from the control panel, and the Zarbi leader guarding them scuttled across to answer it. Doctor Who noted that and moved back to his astral map. He straightened, relaxing.

'Well, it appears we have won another breathing space, my dear.'

'What did you tell them?'

He grinned. 'Nothing. Absolutely nothing!'

'Will you tell them – about the Menoptera?'

'Only as much as I feel I safely can. Come, child, we must appear to be busy.'

'But what are you going to do now . . . to get us all out of here . . .?'

At that Doctor Who halted, thoughtful. He wagged his head slowly, baffled, and said simply. 'Frankly, as yet I have no real idea . . . The answer is' . . . he looked around them 'the answer is . . . here. The power . . . the control – whoever it is that speaks to us . . . all here. But—'

He stroked his chin. Vicki turned, eyeing the Zarbi bustling about their control panel.

'A leader, I suppose – that voice? One of those creatures?'

'I hardly think so. Here – put this recorder back.'

Vicki obeyed, and took the recorder to replace it in a drawer of the control table. She paused at the sight of the specimen glass cases ranged in the drawer and drew one out.

'What did you want with these?' she asked.

'Nothing. Put them away.'

A Zarbi moved towards them and hovered, watching. Its approach startled Vicki and she dropped a glass case. It crashed to the floor and broke. From it rolled a preserved earth specimen – a large spider – a tarantula. It rolled and lay motionless on the floor, its hideous furry legs stiff and unmoving, but the effect on the watching Zarbi and its comrades was extraordinary.

The nearest Zarbi chirruped wildly in alarm and backed hurriedly against a wall. Those nearest to it also reared and scuttled back out of the way, chirruping loudly, all eyes focused on the tarantula. Doctor Who turned at the commotion. Vicki was pointing at the spider, at the Zarbi backing away from it.

'They're frightened, I'm sure of it! Huge evil creatures like them! . . . Doctor – they're frightened!'

Doctor Who's eyes narrowed thoughtfully. He nodded.

Ian ran on, dodging from cover to cover among the rocks and crags, listening for sounds of pursuit, of an alert. He paused to catch his breath, debating which way to go.

Suddenly he lifted his head at a sound he had not heard before. It was a fluttering, a whistling, as of something travelling through the air. He stared about him. As he did so, the Menoptera Vrestin planed down swiftly towards him, his brilliant wings spread, from the vantage point of a crag.

The Menoptera landed, the swiftness of his flight carrying him running towards Ian, his outstretched arms grabbing the young earth man and carrying him on with him. Ian gasped as together they rolled and tumbled down into a dip surrounded by low rocks.

It was not a moment too soon. A loud chirruping now throbbed in the still air and within seconds a swarm of Zarbi was scuttling into view over the landscape, pausing to quest this way and that with their huge glaring eyes. The Zarbi divided and spread out across the landscape, combing it as they went. The chirruping, the scuttling sounds they made over rock and hard grounds, all faded again.

Only then did Vrestin remove the wiry hand he had held firmly clamped over Ian's mouth. Ian stared back at this strangely handsome creature in wonder. Vrestin's straight mouth moved.

'They have gone.' The voice was high-pitched, the accent stilted.

'Who . . . are you?' Almost before he had blurted out the question, the realization struck Ian who this winged creature was.

'You're the . . . Menoptera!'

94

Vrestin nodded. 'And you are . . . from the planet Earth.'

'How do you know?'

Vrestin bowed. 'I have already met one of your party.'

'Barbara. Where is she?

Vrestin paused.

'The Zarbi have her.'

'At this place they call the Crater of Needles?'

Vrestin nodded, and raised a sudden warning hand for silence. He listened, then climbed to the rocks surrounding their hiding-place and peered out. He ducked down as one of their scouts came close by the hollow where they crouched, still looking about, and passed on.

'They are widening the search. We can move on shortly.'

'This Crater of Needles – where is it? How do I get there?'

Vrestin paused. 'Wait and I shall tell you,' he said, watching the Zarbi out of sight.

Ian stared at Vrestin. 'You are the people who are invading this planet?'

Vrestin stiffened. '*Invading* it?' he echoed. 'This is *our* planet! We come to reclaim it! And those of our race who have survived enslavement.'

'But these Zarbi control it. Are you saying *they* are the invaders?'

Vrestin shook his head grimly. 'No. Many generations ago, both our races lived in peace on Vortis. The Zarbi are not an intelligent species – though they were essential to the life pattern here . . .'

'And yet they are now the masters?'

'They became organized, warlike . . . and as they did so – that building back there from which you escaped . . . it . . . just, well, appeared from nowhere – growing, spreading out. We had no weapons – we had never needed them, till then. Too late. They suddenly overran us.'

'So you left the planet?' Ian asked.

'We had no choice. We scratched a bare existence on a planet near Pictos – and planned, multiplied, all for the day when we would return!'

Vrestin rose and peered out again over the rocks.

Ian said, 'And now you're ready?'

'No!' Vrestin said curtly. 'Nowhere near ready. But our elders realized that when the strands of these Zarbi buildings, these webs you see everywhere – when they have joined up across our planet here – we shall have lost forever. Even with such little chance, we *have* to attack. Now!'

'But their tunnels . . . their building . . . their organization. What intelligence brought all that into being? Surely not these Zarbi?'

Vrestin did not answer. He straightened. 'I think it is safe to go now. I will direct you on your journey. I must continue my watch on their headquarters.'

'You? Alone?'

'I am the only survivor of our landing-party. I must render what service I can for our main force, when it lands.'

'What can you do on your own?' Ian protested. 'There are four of our party – two of them inside that headquarters. Help us – and we shall find a way of helping you. The Doctor's wits are more than a match for the Zarbi – or whatever is behind them . . .!'

Ian wished he could be wholly sure of his own boast.

'The . . . Doctor?'

'He is the head of our party. A brilliant man of science, who has travelled infinitely in time and space.'

Vrestin hesitated, doubtful. Ian urged him. 'Take me to this . . . Crater! In return we'll do whatever we can . . . get word to the Doctor . . . glean their secrets, their plans! *You* know the country, but it is *we* who could have the power to help your invasion!'

Vrestin pondered this. He stared across the landscape at the glow of the light from the Zarbi Headquarters. He looked uneasily skyward.

Finally he nodded. 'Perhaps you are right. One alone can perhaps do little. Come. We can risk moving now.'

Vrestin climbed up out of the hollow, looked about him carefully, beckoned to Ian, and led on.

They flitted quietly from the shadow of one crag to another, holding their breath to listen for any alien sound. Vrestin pointed ahead of them.

'No cover there. We shall just have to cross it openly.'

He stepped out, leading the way up a bare rise, ploughing now in sandy ground. At the top he looked down, surveying the landscape ahead. He stretched out a slim hand to the rocky horizon.

'That is the way to the Crater of Needles . . .'

'How far?'

'We should be there in two hours.'

Ian nodded and prepared to follow the tall Menoptera.

Suddenly the humming and the chirruping shattered the silent air. The Zarbi rose out of the soft sand straight ahead of them, rearing their evil heads, and with them a squat, snouted venom grub, too, emerged from its cover of sand and slithered on its multiple legs into position, barring the way.

Ian wheeled. He saw a thin outcrop of rock rising out of the sand away to their right and yelled.

'Over there!'

Vrestin turned and they both raced for its scanty cover, slithering down an incline over the rise.

A Zarbi gestured quickly with its claw. The sting grub spat fire. Sparks skittered off the rocks and an acrid smouldering rose in the air as Ian and Vrestin threw themselves and slid behind their cover. They both stared wildly about and again Ian spotted a fresh refuge.

In the semicircle of rocks a small cave-like opening yawned, partly screened by a drift of sand.

'Vrestin! Here!'

Ian gripped the Menoptera and pulled him, slithering towards the opening as the sand around them now flashed and smouldered under the fire of the venom grub. He urged Vrestin in through the narrow opening and turned for a last look round. He was about to follow the Menoptera in when a choked hollow yell issued from the tiny cave.

'Get back! Get back! The ground's giving way!'

Ian lunged inside, reached out his arm, and yelled back, 'Catch hold of my hand!'

97

Behind him the Zarbi now appeared, their leader directing the gun. Ian felt downward into the opening and found Vrestin's hand. He seized it, but already Vrestin was sliding down out of sight. As Ian hung on grimly he, too, was dragged in through the opening. Vrestin's muffled choking voice came back despairingly.

'Let go – you'll be pulled down with me!'

Still Ian hung on. Vrestin's weight had pulled him entirely into the shallow cave under the rock. As he fought to pull Vrestin back, Ian felt the ground crumble and sink under his weight. Sand cascaded down from the cave walls on either side and suddenly a fissure yawned beneath him. Vrestin's hand was wrenched from his grip. With a wailing cry Vrestin fell down through the dark opening crevasse amid a shower of falling earth.

His cry echoed hollowly back as if from an immense depth before if faded. Ian pulled back now but it was too late. His hands and feet threshed wildly for a hold on firm ground but felt only crumbling sand and emptiness. He slid, and gathering speed fell into a darkness with a wild yell.

At the mouth of the opening under the rocks the Zarbi halted and peered down. Before them a wide fissure now yawned with trickles of sand cascading down it, too deep to see the bottom.

The Zarbi backed hurriedly away from its crumbling edge as the echo of Ian's cry floated upward from its depths.

CHAPTER FOUR

The Crater of Needles

Ian's last memory was of crumbling rock and a deluge of sand cascading all around him as he whirled and fell.

Something hit him and it seemed that the back of his head opened and let in an explosion of light and pain.

His consciousness faded like a rocket, trailing fire.

There was an eternity of darkness before the shadows lightened – and very slowly, muttering and relapsing into sleep, he finally awoke. He blinked hard. His head was one great throbbing ache. He moved painfully on to an elbow.

Near him a shape stirred and moaned and he turned, touched it.

It was Vrestin. Ian reached and shook him. The Menopter's eyes fluttered, opened slightly.

'It seemed ... we were falling ... forever ...' Vrestin mumbled, then suddenly sat up and stared around.

'This place – what is it?'

The rough walls glowed with colour. When Ian focused his eyes he saw they were designs – decorations – gaudy and brilliant enough to rival the colouring of Vrestin's own splendid wings.

A greenish light pervaded this place. They were in a rocky underground chamber, smooth-floored except for a scatter of small rocks and sand about them which had accompanied their fall.

Vrestin looked up – and sure enough, a gap showed in the roof of the cave.

'We must have fallen through that.'

'I'm taking a look round,' Ian said.

He got up stiffly. As he did so he heard a rush of feet – and stopped dead.

99

Several shadows launched themselves at him from the corner of the room. The eerie light glittered on the weapons which they thrust forward at Ian and Vrestin, now rising dizzily to his feet.

It was hard to see the faces behind the thicket of spears which suddenly hemmed them in, immovable, staring around them.

The Crater of Needles was a vast, flat depression in the land. The horizon on all sides was rimmed by high, jagged rocks.

From its level floor hundreds of slender stalagmites rose sheer and high like multiple glass spires, and the ground between was dotted with acid pools, giving off their vaporous fumes. Something like vegetation remained here – scattered stumps of petrified trees.

On one of the high rocks, a Zarbi, holding in control the humped shape of a venom grub, surveyed the scene below with its large, shining eyes.

A small army toiled beneath on the floor of the crater, watched by guards. They were felling the brittle, petrified tree trunks and breaking off the smaller mica stalagmites, chipping wearily away at them with heavy implements. The workers were grimy and ragged. Their wings were dull and short-clipped, but otherwise they resembled the more colourful Menoptera.

These were the remains of the Menoptera race which had been left on Vortis. They had been enslaved by the conquering Zarbi. Near by stood their primitive huts built between the tree trunks and the spar stumps of the broken stalagmites.

The brilliantly coloured Hrostar stood out among this grimy mass of slaves. Though a prisoner, he walked with dignity, unhurried, bearing a bundle of broken stalagmite spars. At the brink of an acid pool he paused for a moment, tired. The Zarbi guard on the pool chirruped and gestured angrily. Hrostar glared and then, stubbornly taking his time, emptied the spars into the pool. A puff of acrid smoke swirled up.

Near him an old slave Menoptera came staggering towards

the pool, breathing heavily under his burden of spars. Hrostar halted him with a gesture.

'You are too old to carry such a burden, Prapillus,' he said. 'Let me take it.'

'I am fitter than many half my age,' the old man retorted testily, clinging to his bundle and stumping on towards the pool.

'My father is very stubborn,' a voice said. Hrostar turned. A Menoptera girl, Hlynia, was looking at him. She smiled. Though her winged finery was tarnished and soiled, she was beautiful.

'Not stubborn – proud', Hrostar said gently.

Barbara came toiling towards them with a load of spars. She was exhausted, and she stumbled and fell. Not until a Zarbi guard turned and chirruped menacingly did she gather enough strength to rise. Hrostar bent and helped her gather the spars. She looked around her wearily.

'Hrostar – what is this work we are doing for?'

Hrostar held up a spar. 'Raw materials for the Zarbi buildings.' He tossed an armful of spars into the acid pool and watched the smoke rise. 'These are drawn into the centre, through underground streams. As we load them in – the building reaches out across Vortis.'

'This centre – this . . . building – that's where the Doctor will be,' Barbara mused. 'I'm sure of it.'

'At the Zarbi Headquarters?'

Again their Zarbi guard chirruped and raised a threatening foreclaw. Hurriedly Barbara collected the rest of the spars and fed them into the pool. She and Hrostar turned and tracked tiredly back for another load. Barbara was thoughtful.

She said, 'Somehow I shall have to try and make my way there . . .'

'To the Headquarters of the Zarbi? Impossible!'

'Is it?' Barbara asked, defiantly.

'A girl alone? Do you imagine you can succeed where a dozen of our Menoptera scouts failed?' Hrostar turned and gestured to the toiling slaves. 'We landed here to liberate our

own folk. We know this planet better than you. Yet we met disaster, Vrestin, myself and the others. The Zarbi were everywhere. They captured our guns. We were trying to contact our spearhead, waiting out in space, when the Zarbi burst into the cave. We had to smash our communicator. And now . . .' Hrostar shrugged helplessly.

'This spearhead force of yours – when does it arrive?' Barbara asked.

Hrostar was about to answer when he checked himself warily. He turned away. 'Soon,' he said curtly.

'Will the invasion succeed?'

'It *must*! The Zarbi Headquarters building has got to be destroyed, or we shall lose Vortis forever!'

'But if the Zarbi are so powerful, how will you overcome them?'

'We have a new weapon. Our scientists have been working to perfect it. If it fulfils their hopes, it will sweep these vile creatures from Vortis.'

'What is this weapon?' asked Barbara.

Hrostar hesitated, doubtful whether he should confide in Barbara, a stranger.

'If we ever get near enough to the Zarbi Headquarters with it – you will see what it does,' he said.

Doctor Who and Vicki were staring at the small slow-moving mass of light spots on the astral map.

The Doctor straightened, nodded.

'Yes, I'd say definitely – a space army. And on the move, too.'

Behind them a Zarbi entered the control room from one of the webbed tunnels. Vicki turned and noted it was carrying a strange tubular object. Its muzzle was ringed with small clusters of tubes, and at the wider stock end it held a panel of buttons like a typewriter keyboard.

Vicki nudged the Doctor and pointed it out furtively as the Zarbi laid the instrument near a pile of the gold wishbone necklets.

'What's that thing it's got?

Doctor Who peered sidelong at the Zarbi and the object it was examining before laying it down.

'Mm – looks like some sort of weapon, child ...'

He returned to his calculations.

'Yes, but what sort – it's nothing like these creatures could make, surely?

'That's true – no.'

The Doctor pondered that, until a fresh burst of hummed instructions came from the Zarbis' control panel and the great light above the web indicator glowed. The Zarbi manning it chirruped and rose to attention.

Then the Dome in the roof began to descend.

Vicki began to back away. The Zarbi had laid down the gun and was now coming towards her with a necklet levelled at her throat.

'No ...!' she moaned. 'No ... no ...'

Doctor Who stepped in the Zarbi's way. 'What is it you want?' he stormed. The Zarbi extended a foreclaw and thrust the Doctor roughly aside. It seized the shrinking Vicki and clamped the necklet roughly about her throat. Doctor Who wheeled and strode angrily towards the descending Dome. He stood beneath it, lifted his head, and raged into it.

'What is the meaning of this? I demand the child be set free! Is this the way you reward us for our help?'

The Voice boomed back. 'It is the way we reward your lack of it! You have had time to present the information you spoke of, yet still you delay! To teach you obedience, the child will die!'

The Doctor stiffened and shouted back. 'If the child dies, I shall have no reason left to obey you! I have located your enemy. My calculations are complete ...'

'You lie-ie!' The echo of the Voice's anger surged around the Doctor deafeningly. He paused, knowing now that he must yield some information to bargain for Vicki's safety.

'I am telling the truth! Your enemy are massing in the vicinity of the planet Pictos ...'

A pause. Then ...

'Pictos-os ...?'

'They are one hundred and forty leagues from this planet ... and moving closer ...'

'How quickly-y ...?'

'At one-tenth the speed of light. Now if you wish to waste your time with idle stupid vengeance on a child in the face of invasion – you will be annihilated!'

After another pause the Dome reverberated to a question from the Voice, now calmer.

'Where will the Menoptera land ... and ...?'

Doctor Who hesitated now, reluctant to reveal any more. He cast an anxious look towards Vicki, now blank of face, standing unaware before the threat of a venom grub which was now being guided towards her by a Zarbi guard. The Doctor looked up into the Dome.

'Your interference has so far prevented my finding that out. If we are spared further treatment of this sort, I can return to the task you set me – if it is not too late!'

There was a silence while the Voice digested this.

'Very well – go!'

Doctor Who stood his ground. 'Not before the child is released!'

'Go – immediately!'

'First, the child –!'

The Zarbi controlling the venom gun turned towards the control panel. It hummed, glowed suddenly. The Zarbi snatched the necklet from Vicki's throat and the Dome rose into the air. Doctor Who took Vicki's arm and steered her towards his control table as she rubbed her eyes and awoke.

'What ... did you tell ... that thing ...?' Vicki mumbled.

Doctor Who smiled. 'Only enough to preserve our skins, my dear.' He patted her arm, turned to his map, and then muttered, thinking.

'We must think of something to get away from here. Vicki – the recorder – we must find somewhere to hide it.'

'Why?'

'Because I don't intend to present them with *all* the information we've picked up on it ... where they are to be attacked, for instance ...'

Doctor Who paused, wondering where to conceal the recorder, when the Zarbi control panel again burst into life. Lights glowed from different points on the web indicator, buzzers of different pitch sounded through speaker lines beneath the map, and the master speaker hummed loudly with a steady flow of instructions. The Zarbi operating the control panel were chirruping excitedly in response. Vicki watched all this.

She said, 'There's another panic on – look!'

Doctor Who nodded grimly. 'They're putting their army on the alert, no doubt. They didn't take long, you see, to act on what I did tell them!'

Suddenly the slaves toiling in the Crater of Needles stopped and looked up and around them.

Warning hooters were sounding all along the crater rim. There was frenzied activity among their Zarbi guards, who were scuttling down from their vantage points in the rocks to assemble information – then hurrying off in directions pointed out by their leaders.

'What is it?' Barbara asked. 'Some kind of alarm?'

Hrostar was listening, watching everything keenly. He glanced at the sky anxiously.

'Yes. I hope they haven't found . . .' Hrostar didn't finish the sentence. Several Zarbi guards came scuttling down to the clearing where they worked. Prapillus saw them first.

'Look out,' the old Menoptera said. 'They're bringing their stings with them.'

'Stings . . .?' Barbara was bewildered.

Hrostar pointed at the evil venom grubs with their long deadly projectile snouts. 'Venom grubs,' he said curtly. 'They can spit death as far as a cannon.'

The 'stings' halted at a sign from the Zarbi, covering the slaves. The Zarbi reared and waved at the slaves, pointing towards the crude prison huts.

'They want us to go to our huts,' Hrostar said.

The weary slaves downed their tools and responded slowly. The Zarbi harried them angrily, urgently, to move more quickly. As the slaves crowded into their prison huts the sting grubs turned, keeping them covered.

Hrostar paused inside the door of their hut and remained there looking out cautiously. A sting under the control of a Zarbi guard remained pointing at their door. The other Zarbi were climbing back to join the squads marshalling on the crater rim.

Old Prapillus hobbled forward to join Hrostar's anxious watch. He stared outward and ventured a question.

'Hrostar – it is the invasion, do you think?'

Hrostar stared upward uneasily. 'The spearhead, yes, I think so . . .'

'Then tell us what we must do!' The old Menoptera said excitedly.

Hrostar paused. 'Nothing!' he said. 'Not yet . . .'

A discontented mutter arose among the expectant slaves. Hlynia, Prapillus' beautiful daughter, turned indignantly on Hrostar.

'Do *nothing*? We have waited generations for this moment!'

Hrostar did not answer. He pondered and paced restlessly.

He muttered, 'The spearhead was intended to create a bridgehead for the main force. It was to be a complete surprise. He stared outward. 'If this is an alert – how did the Zarbi know?'

Suddenly a thought struck him. He turned suspiciously on Barbara, pointed at her. 'Your earth friends! This man of science you tell me of – could *he* be helping them?'

Barbara, taken aback, hesitated uncertainly. 'Well . . . no!' she protested. 'I'm . . . I'm sure he wouldn't . . .!'

'If they have captured him, as they did you, they could *make* him help!'

'The Doctor would not give in easily,' Barbara said stoutly.

Hrostar shook his head, unconvinced. 'They are powerful! They have uncanny means of persuasion.' He turned to Prapillus. 'Prapillus – do you know the Sayo Plateau?'

Prapillus nodded. 'Of course. It borders on this crater.'

Hrostar stared. 'Here? Then they *do* know!'

'Know what?' Barbara asked.

Hrostar fretted and paced to and fro like a caged animal.

'Our spearhead planned to land on Sayo Plateau!' he said. He pointed out towards the sting which covered their hut unwaveringly.' And with these Zarbi weapons – they will be massacred!'

'But your force will be armed!' Barbara argued.

Hrostar hesitated. 'Not sufficiently to deal with the hosts of the Zarbi. We aimed to land in secret – and to destroy the building which *controls* them! Everything depended on surprise, secrecy. And now . . . the Zarbi know!'

Prapillus and his daughter Hlynia had been conferring with the slaves crowded in the back of the hut. Now they came forward.

Prapillus said gravely, 'Then your spearhead must be warned.'

Hrostar shrugged helplessly. 'How? The Zarbi smashed our signalling equipment!'

Barbara had an idea. 'Then we must get to the plateau . . . intercept them . . . warn them . . . !'

Prapillus nodded. 'Exactly.'

Hrostar pointed outside. 'But there is a sting-gun pointed straight at this door. Powerful enough to kill everyone in this hut, the moment we make a move!'

'I'm aware of that,' Prapillus said impatiently.

Hlynia was staring outside towards the crater rim. She turned back. 'But they have taken most of the Zarbi from this outpost.'

'Which leaves this crater undermanned, with only a few guards!' Barbara said. 'Hrostar – we've got to distract the Zarbi who are left . . . draw them away . . . and escape!'

Hrostar was pondering the venom grub pointing immovably at their hut door. 'If only we could destroy that sting!' he exclaimed.

Prapillus nodded. 'I may do that', he said simply.

The others stared. 'You . . . how?' Hrostar said.

The old man tapped his head wisely and smiled. He moved towards the back of the hut and began to move their stored food supply – crude jars of preserved nectar, roots, piles of dried nuts – from the shelves.

'I know the Zarbi,' Prapillus grunted. 'I have studied their habits all my life. *They* are not our natural enemies. It is the thing which controls them which we must destroy. Without it, the Zarbi are useless ... powerless. Come, help me ...'

And Prapillus began to break a hole in the side of the hut. As he worked he called Hrostar to his side.

'Place some of my people near the front of the hut. Tell them to act naturally, take no notice of what we are doing. We do not want the Zarbi to suspect anything.'

Hrostar did as he was asked, silently marshalling others in the hut nearer to the door. Prapillus motioned to those nearest him to help with the hole. Soon they had torn a cavity big enough to crawl through.

The old man cocked an ear towards the distant sounds of chirruping. He bent double and prepared to crawl through the hole, then paused. He turned to Hrostar, Hlynia and Barbara, and his eyes twinkled.

'Do not be surprised at anything you hear,' he said. 'Watch the sting grub – and wait your chance.'

'But, Father ...!'

'Do not worry for me, Hlynia, child. I may be a little short of breath, but not of brains.'

The old Menoptera touched his daughter's hand and disappeared through the hole in the wall. Hrostar stared through it and watched him go. Then he straightened.

'He's disappeared out of sight,' he said. But he continued to watch.

The Zarbi manning the sting grub suddenly turned its huge sleek head. It had heard a crackle, like something falling among the stalagmites away to the right – and it fixed its shining stare on a shape flitting among them.

Swiftly the Zarbi raised a pointing foreclaw and the murderous sting of the venom grub swivelled to follow it.

The shape disappeared.

Prapillus dodged nimbly and crouched low among the stalagmite needles. He waited, then cupped his hands to his mouth.

A high-pitched chirruping sounded, uncannily like the language of the Zarbi.

The Zarbi guard manning the sting grub started at the sound. It left the sting motionless and scuttled a few paces forward towards the stalagmites. The chirruping sounded again, ahead of the Zarbi, and it answered on a questioning note, expecting to see a comrade detach itself from among the rocks.

Inside the hut Hrostar was now staring out of the doorway. He turned back to the others.

'It's left the sting – now's our chance!'

He moved swiftly to the shelf-like bunks and took down a handful of spars.

'What can we do?' Barbara asked.

'Help me destroy it!' Hrostar handed around the slender but heavy lumps of stalagmite.

'Destroy it? Couldn't *we* control it – use it ourselves?'

Hrostar shook his head. 'Only the Zarbi can control and fire those beasts.' He strode to the door, looked out. He motioned to his companions and muttered, 'Get ready – I'll give the command . . .!'

Again, crouched in his hiding-place among the stalagmite needles, Prapillus cupped his hands and chirruped. He watched the Zarbi guard approach, head questing this way and that, and chuckled. The old man was enjoying his role hugely. He turned on his hands and knees and crawled farther away. He heard the Zarbi challenge him now with an angry chirrup. He grinned – and again paused to call back, mockingly.

Watching from within the hut doorway, Hrostar suddenly exclaimed, 'Now!'

He darted forward and out. Barbara followed, then Hlynia. As they came out into the clearing before the hut, the Zarbi turned and saw them. It broke into an angry, jabbering chirrup, raising its foreclaw swiftly – and the sting gun turned and began to bear on the three friends as they rushed out of the hut.

Before it could fire, a shadow rose out of the ground behind the Zarbi. It was Prapillus. With the agility of a monkey the old man leaped on the creature's back and bore it staggering to the ground. As it did so, Barbara and Hlynia rushed the venom creature, their spars raised like clubs. At the same time Hrostar leaped to aid the old Menoptera. Before the Zarbi could recover, it was felled with a mighty blow from a spar, then another, and another, leaving it stunned and

almost motionless on its back, its limbs waving faintly, feebly.

The venom-gun, powerless without the controlling influence of its Zarbi master, crumpled under the spars of Barbara and Hlynia and lay twitching on its side. Hrostar and Prapillus joined them.

'Good work!' Hrostar panted.

Barbara turned to the old Menoptera, Prapillus.

'His was the good work. None of *us* could have done it.'

Prapillus tapped his head and chuckled. They looked about them for a sign of any other Zarbi.

'Come!' Hlynia said. 'I can lead you to the plateau.' She hurried ahead. With a last look about them at the jerking, helpless Zarbi and the crushed sting creature, Barbara and Hrostar moved to follow her.

Ian and Vrestin stood hemmed in by the spears levelled at their throats by the silent beings who had rushed to surround them as they recovered from their fall.

The weapons held at their throats were strangely twisted, like huge corkscrews, with murderously sharp tips, and behind these the eyes of their captors glittered. No sound came from them.

Ian's eyes took in more clearly the slanting, highly decorated walls around them.

Vrestin was also taking stock of the place, and the creatures who crowded around, holding them at bay.

'It's some kind of a nest!' Vrestin exclaimed.

Ian peered at the creatures behind the strange spears. As his eyes became used to the gloom he saw that they were not unlike the Menoptera. They were smaller – dwarfed, in fact, by the tall Vrestin – and paler of skin. Their eyes were narrow, and they lacked the gaudy Menoptera markings. Also, they had no wings – only stumps, which hunched their backs. But they were alert, quick, and venomously hostile as they pressed Ian and Vrestin back against a wall with their spears and silently held them there.

Then one of their number thrust through and pointed. At that the thicket of spears jabbed at Ian and Vrestin, forcing them to turn and stumble along a short corridor between the brightly painted walls.

Hustled by the jabbing spears, the earth man and the tall Menoptera staggered down into a large chamber daubed with bright markings.

Ian stared ahead of him and saw they were being forced towards a wall of smoke.

The smoke wreathed upward into the chamber from a

crevice in the floor. A crude cauldron was suspended over this great fissure, filled with a thick, gluey liquid which bubbled and spat. At the sight of this Ian halted, resisting the jabbing which drove them forward, and yelled desperately.

'We mean you no harm! Vrestin – tell them!'

Vrestin walked stiffly and proudly beside him, sparing their captors a disdainful glare. He said loftily, 'They do not believe me any more than you!'

As they were forced in front of the smoking cauldron Ian peered downward. He saw a ruddy molten glow far beneath him and felt the heat which swirled up through the crevasse.

'There's a flame down there! It's a crack in the planet's crust.'

They halted. The thicket of spears behind them parted and one of their captors came through. He was small and alert, and surveyed them through slitted eyes. He turned and gestured with a delicate hand to the cauldron. To Ian's astonishment, he spoke – in a high, cracked voice, weirdly accented. 'Place your hands in there!'

Ian exchanged a startled glance with Vrestin – who, in spite of his lofty contempt of these creatures, was clearly surprised. Suddenly Ian felt his arms seized and he struggled wildly, wincing and giving a groan as a spear jabbed mercilessly into his side. He was borne, fighting, feet dragging to the brim of the cauldron – and there a dozen creatures gripped him, locked his hands together, and plunged them into the seething liquid.

He flinched against the expected agony of terrible scalding, and then his face cleared wonderingly.

'It's just . . . warm . . .!' he muttered in relief.

Vrestin was subjected to the same treatment. The pigmy-like creatures brought Ian's hands out, now dripping with the gluey wax.

'. . . a sort of gum! What for?'

He tried to free his hands. They were stuck tight, clamped in a ball of substance that was quickly hardening. Suddenly Ian understood its purpose. He shrugged.

'Ah, well – better than handcuffs, I suppose . . .'

But the proud Vrestin was resisting and storming scornfully. 'Barbarians! What is it that you want with us?'

The creature who had directed this operation gestured again and uttered an order in his cracked sing-song.

'Over here . . .!'

The spears urged Vrestin and Ian to their feet and they were forced towards a rough seat. They were shoved on to it, surrounded by spears while one of the creatures ladled some more of the wax from the cauldron and approached.

He poured this around Ian's ankles, patting it into a solid, rock-hard lump as it cooled.

During all this one of their captors, heavily lined about its narrow eyes and appearing infinitely older than its companions now moved forward, and the thicket of spears parted respectfully to allow him through.

'Make way for Hetra!' the leader with the cracked voice ordered.

The aged creature who had been called Hetra drew himself up, with some dignity, and stared at Ian and Vrestin.

'We will test your reasons for entering our nest,' he announced, in a hollow voice that trembled with age. He turned and beckoned to the other leader, then pointed to three of their guards.

'A trial?' Ian said. 'Without listening to *us*?'

Hetra halted and turned. He gave Ian a look of withering mistrust. 'You would not tell the truth – so your appearance is unnecessary. If we consider you hostile, and enemies – you will die!'

The creature they called Hetra gestured to those of his companions he had chosen and stalked away.

In the control room of the Zarbi Headquarters there was now such furious activity that the guards ignored the presence of Doctor Who and Vicki. The Zarbi manning the control panel were busy relaying streams of instructions to all sections of the planet. This was clear as they flicked different controls, and lights glowed on different segments of the web indicator.

In silence, Doctor Who nudged Vicki. He held a finger

to his lips and signed to her to watch the distracted Zarbi control room operators.

Then keeping his own eye on the distant control panel, Doctor Who stole sidelong glances towards the heap of wishbone necklets a guard had piled on the floor not far from them. He reached it without attracting attention and cautiously bent towards the pile.

With a pencil between his outstretched fingers, the Doctor carefully lifted a necklet, balancing it with difficulty and taking care that it should not touch his skin. Suddenly his eye lit on the strange gun-like weapon he had seen a Zarbi bring into the Headquarters and lay down. He stretched and reached for the gun, too.

Now, while Vicki watched the Zarbi with her breath held, Doctor Who tiptoed back towards their astral table. There, with a sly smile of triumph, he tipped the necklet off his pencil on to the table, then dropped a paper over it as a shield from the gaze of any inquisitive Zarbi who might wander near. He cast a look over his shoulder.

'Let's hope they leave us alone long enough for me to complete these tests,' he said to Vicki.

He peered closely at the necklet, puzzled, thoughtful. Then he appeared to make up his mind. He reached and brought over a small box with a dial on it, graduated, not with figures, but with segments of different colours. He held this near the necklet, watched the needle flicker, took a reading as the needle stopped in a segment of the dial coloured in blue. He jotted down a note on a pad, muttered.

'Hmm . . . they are controlled by . . . that . . .'

And the Doctor turned his eye towards the Dome now hanging high up on the roof. He looked back at the necklet.

'. . . and in turn . . . control others . . .'

'How, Doctor?' Vicki asked.

Doctor Who straightened, hopeful now, 'When I know that, my dear, well . . . sauce for the goose may be . . . sauce for the gander . . . I wonder . . .'

And he beamed mysteriously at a puzzled Vicki, without deigning to explain more.

'How do you mean?'

'Shh, child – keep watch on those creatures while I work.'

Now, feverishly, the Doctor opened drawers in the table and selected odd pieces of equipment, transformers, condensers, valves. He began busily connecting these, snipping wires, joining, until he had fashioned a strange electronic contraption and concentrated on connecting it by wire with the wishbone necklet.

Then, with an eye on the Zarbi, the Doctor moved around the table, unhooked the leads connecting it to *Tardis* and its power system – and plugged these into the strange circuit he had built.

He paused, his hand hovering doubtfully over the contraption's switch. He cast a look back towards the ship.

'Now we know the *Tardis* is an opposing force to the power in this Headquarters ... that's why that gun kicked back. Question is – which force is the stronger ...?'

Vicki eyed the necklet, the small circlet of gold which had already shown such power. She said uncertainly, 'What would happen if ... this force here, the Zarbi's ... is stronger ...?'

Doctor Who shrugged a little uneasily. 'Then I'm afraid the ship's mechanism will be ruined – ruined. However, we have no choice. Stand back, Vicki ...'

Abruptly he pressed down the switch.

There was a crackle, a small sharp flash from the necklet.

Doctor Who looked pleased. He paused, then snatched up the necklet in his bare hands. 'Look – harmless! I've done it.' He chuckled and slipped the necklet back on to the table.

But the sound had alerted the Zarbi. They chirruped, and one of their number over at the control panel came scurrying towards Doctor Who and Vicki.

At the sight of the creature bearing down on her Vicki lost her head a little. She snatched up the recorder and showed it.

'It was ... nothing ... just ... a, uh ... fuse on one of our instruments ...'

Doctor Who stared in dismay. He snatched the precious

recorder as the Zarbi reached for it and slipped it into a pocket. The central Dome was descending from the roof and the Zarbi, in the act of seizing Doctor Who turned, sighted the Dome, and obediently thrust the Doctor reeling towards it.

The Voice was booming already before it closed over his silvery head. It was thundering menacingly, '. . . ample time to complete your findings-ings! . . . Report-ort . . .!!'

'They are not yet complete,' the Doctor lied calmly.

'That is a reply you constantly use-se!' The Voice raged. 'No doubt your creatures reported the explosion – a defect on my instruments due to this continual force interference! Blame your own power for these delays, for having to wait, not me . . .!

Vicki could see Doctor Who inside the Dome but could not hear the words with which the old man tried to keep bluffing his questioner. What alarmed Vicki was the sight of the Zarbi who now turned and scurried for the control panel, where it chirruped messages into a speaker. The central light of the web glowed hugely in answer – and then went out.

Inside the Dome an ominous silence now fell. The Voice did not answer Doctor Who's protestations. He fidgeted and snapped, 'so if you want our help, I repeat – turn off your power, or, or be prepared to wait . . .!'

There was still no answer.

'Well?' the Doctor challenged.

Finally the Voice replied, almost quietly, but on a new and chilling note.

It said, 'I have been infrormed that you pocketed some equipment. I have been informed . . .'

'Quite so, yes – a piece of equipment damaged during my uh, tests . . .'

His voice trailed off as an alarming noise now sounded and echoed around the Dome – a low-pitched throbbing, rising to an intense hum. Then to his amazement the noise of a transmitter opened up.

It was coming from the recorder in his hand!

Now the voices he had recorded intoned, repeating the

messages he had picked up ... 'course on bearing two-six-five. Spéed point owe-one of light. We jettison craft at altitude two-five leagues ...'

Doctor Who stared speechless at the recorder. Desperately he jammed at a switch to cut it off. But it continued, entirely unaffected.

'... individual descent to group on Sayo Plateau ... at northern extremity of Crater of Needles ...'

The transmitter sound and the voice with it faded and cut off as the message ceased. A deathly silence followed. Then the Voice boomed with harsh triumph.

'You were in possession of the information all the time-me! You will be dealt with when the invasion has been repelled-elled ...!'

Abruptly the Dome lifted and rose away to the roof. Doctor Who turned and stared. He and Vicki were surrounded on all sides by glaring Zarbi.

It was useless to resist. Neither he nor Vicki could take a pace in any direction.

One of the Zarbi held two necklets. It levelled these, thrust them forward. Doctor Who fought to keep his consciousness but his eyes glazed, and he and Vicki stood suddenly motionless, in a trance. The Zarbi pointed with its foreclaw. Obediently the Doctor and Vicki turned and walked dazedly towards a wall. They stood there, their eyes wide but unseeing.

One Zarbi remained to watch them, reared on its hind legs.

Now the control panel burst into action with a fresh stream of hummed orders, and with the great central light glowing. The Zarbi operators turned and scurried to obey its summons.

Clearly the Intelligence which controlled them had triumphed. It had secured all the information it needed.

Now it was acting, and issuing its battle orders.

Gripped tightly by the hardened gum which held their hands and feet in this weird nest far below ground, Ian and Vrestin sat staring around them at their captors, waiting. Ian strained his ears to hear the mutter of conversation from this odd tribunal of creatures who had captured them and now sat in a neighbouring chamber, debating their fate.

He could make nothing of their words. His look turned towards their guards who ringed them in a circle a few paces away. Vrestin was also looking around him with puzzled curiosity. He wagged his head, baffled.

'I can't understand it,' he muttered.

Ian growled. 'You refuse to admit that such grubby, undersized little creatures as these could be related to the great race of Menoptera! Is it because you're proud, or simply blind!'

Vrestin stared at Ian. He peered more keenly at the stunted guards who watched them from a distance. At length he nodded a little unwillingly.

'But no Menoptera would live *under* the ground,' he protested. 'They would rather be slaves! Yet . . . they could be of our species . . . another race, but . . . still, a kind of Menoptera.'

'Have you no idea how such a race could have come here, down into a foul place like this . . . or from where?' Ian asked.

Vrestin shook his head. 'There are no records of our flight from Vortis. It was long ago, before my time. Many fell to their death – but I cannot think how or where *these* kind came from . . .'

'Well, blood relatives or not, they're your enemies now! And unless we can persuade them differently, they are at this very moment discussing how they are going to kill us!' Ian motioned savagely towards the next chamber from which a subdued mutter of talk issued.

Vrestin was pondering that. 'There just may be . . . a way . . . of explaining . . . how they came to be here . . .' he mused.

There was a scuffling of feet from the neighbouring room as the council ended. The guards parted their ranks to make way first for the aged leader, Hetra, and his lieutenants.

They came to Ian and Vrestin and stopped before them. There was a grave silence.

Hetra spoke.

'The decision has been reached,' he announced in his high-pitched quaver. 'Every creature who invades our domain comes only to prey on us. You are guilty ...' He beckoned to his deputy. 'Nemini ...?'

The stunted creature called Nemini stepped forward. His slitted eyes glittered as he surveyed both Ian and Vrestin. He clapped his hands and several guards seized the Earth man and the Menoptera. Nemini pointed to the smoking fissure over which the cauldron hung.

'Throw them into the fire chasm!'

Ian threw off the hands that grabbed him, wheeled to face Hetra, and yelled, pointing at Vrestin, 'This man is your own kind! Are you going to *murder* him?'

Nemini and the guards halted a moment, gaping, and looked to their leader. Hetra stared towards Vrestin who had drawn himself erect, staring contemptuously around him.

'This stranger?' Hetra said with scorn. He pointed upward. 'You are both from that wilderness above ground, where the light blinds, the air chokes, where only destroyer races live, where none of us who has gone forth has ever returned.' He levelled a shaking finger first at Ian, then at Vrestin. 'You come foraging into our world only for new victims! Take them!'

As the guards leaped forward and overpowered them, Vrestin shouted.

'Listen! The wilderness you speak of up there belongs to you! We are coming in our legions to free this planet of its killers – the Zarbi! It's they who are your enemies ...!'

But resist as he might, their tiny captors dragged Ian and Vrestin to the brink of the precipice, and as they stared down, the flames and molten glow from far below lit their faces.

The guards turned to await the signal from their leader – but Hetra was frowning, puzzling over Vrestin's words, gazing into a distance as if at a memory ... or a vision. He held up a frail hand, and his narrow eyes sought Vrestin's questioningly.

'The ... Zarbi ...?' Hetra quavered.

'They seized this place fifty generations ago!' Vrestin retorted. 'They enslaved your forbears and mine who remained. They are spreading their poisonous web to every corner of Vortis!'

Nemini interrupted, waving an impatient hand. He turned a mistrustful glare on the two prisoners and shouted, pointing to the fire chasm, 'As long as we deal with intruders thus, we are safe here! Come ...!'

Ian rounded on him. 'Can't you understand? You are the Menoptera! Like him!'

He pointed at Vrestin and then checked. A sudden total hush had fallen. The eyes of the entire company of their captors had turned on him in awe.

Hetra broke the silence. 'The ... Menoptera?' he asked.

Nemini glared. 'You blaspheme! You are talking of our gods!' he stormed, raising a spear.

'Your gods?' Vrestin echoed, astonished. 'The Menoptera are your *kinsmen!*' He reached out among their guards, now standing, stunned, like statues – and whirled one of them round with a thrust of his arm. He pointed at the stumps which sprouted from the creature's narrow shoulders.

'Your wings have withered on your bodies, while you crawled blindly underground like so many pupae. You were born to the greatest freedom of all creatures – to light, to beauty, and to peace!'

As these ringing words sunk in, their guards exchanged wondering glances, half-sensing the possibility that they might be the truth.

'But ...' the aged Hetra protested feebly. 'It is death ... for us ... up there ...'

Vrestin gestured around him. 'What is this place for you – but a *living* death? This is not your element!'

As their captors now hesitated and muttered among themselves Ian shouted, 'If you throw us into the fire chasm you destroy your own future! ... and condemn yourselves to skulk down here forever!'

Nemini wheeled to challenge them both. 'Prove what you say!' he demanded.

Vrestin drew himself up, towering above their guards, staring haughtily around him.

'I am Vrestin, a leader of the Menoptera. You are our

kin! We come to rid this planet of a creature which has it in its grip!'

'... and we need your help!' Ian added.

There was an abrupt rustle, a great swish of sound. Hetra, Nemini and all their fellow creatures were now staring past Ian in fascination and awe.

He turned. He saw that Vrestin now stood before them with his arms outflung and his magnificent wings unfolded, stretched to their full magnificent beauty for the first time

At this rich and inspiring sight, some of their guards had staggered back and were standing with their heads hung – bowing before the Menoptera leader in his gaudy splendour.

A long winding climb among rough and little-used paths had brought Barbara, Hrostar, Hlynia and her father Prapillus out of the Crater of Needles at its northern tip until they could pause, crouched and breathless, in the shelter of a circle of rocks, and survey the tableland that now came into view.

'The Sayo Plateau,' Hlynia whispered, pointing.

They waited, scanning the sky anxiously, listening for any sound.

The satellites hung above the horizon, glowing, motionless against the pale vault of space. The silence was complete. There was not even the remotest sound of Zarbi in the area.

'I ... can't hear a thing,' Barbara said. 'Surely the Zarbi—'

'—Listen!' Hrostar commanded them sharply.

They halted, straining their ears – and then they heard it. A great swooping sound planed over their heads. They turned their eyes quickly in the direction from which it came.

Hrostar stiffened. 'They're landing!' he exclaimed.

Barbara wheeled towards the exit from their rock shelter and called, 'Let's get on to the plateau – we'll stand a better chance of warning them from there ...'

The others moved quickly to follow her. As they did so a mighty beating of wings sounded all around them – like the passage of a great swarm of huge birds. As Barbara looked up, she saw the shadowy shapes of Menoptera planing down, running to a halt before them on the plateau, and turning this way and that, questing where to go.

Right in front of her a Menoptera dropped out of the sky. It saw Barbara and brought up its gun. She ran towards it stumbling over the wavy ground. As she halted to call a greeting, she froze. A great humming and chirruping had broken out all around them. There was a sheet of flame and the Menoptera facing her only a few paces ahead spun around and crumpled, his body smoking from the deadly jet of a sting-gun.

As Barbara and Hrostar turned to look wildly this way and that they saw the shapes of the Zarbi creeping over the hillocks, bordering the plateau, guiding their sting grubs like so many avenging hunting dogs. As the first jets of venom burst among the descending fighters, the Menoptera swooping to land on the plateau flattened themselves in a desperate search for cover and levelled their own guns.

The blast of a Zarbi gun seared Barbara's ears and a Menoptera running towards their shelter screamed. Now the Zarbi fire crackled and flashed all around them, and Barbara, Hlynia and Prapillus could only press themselves back into the shadow of their rock shelter and watch the battle out on the plateau in horror.

'An ambush!' Barbara breathed.

'I must help them!' Hrostar yelled and plunged towards his newly arrived comrades. Barbara clutched at him and held on desperately, shouting, 'You will only get yourself killed! You haven't even a gun! You can do nothing!'

A swoop sounded above them. They looked up and the figure of a Menoptera alighted on a crag, staring down at Barbara and the others. Hrostar sighted it and cried, 'Spearhead!'

The figure levelled a gun and rapped back.

'Codeword?'

'Electron!' Hrostar answered.

The Menoptera officer surveyed them, stared about him. 'Where is your pilot party?'

'Destroyed!' Hrostar shouted back. 'Your force – get it off the plateau!'

The Menoptera astride the crag glared grimly towards the fighting. 'Why?' he demanded.

'Our combat weapons are useless. The Zarbi have our rendezvous. Disperse the spearhead, or they will be massacred!'

'It's too late. We are committed to attack!'

'Look!' Barbara screamed, pointing out beyond their

124

shelter. The shapes of the Zarbi now stood out on top of every rock fringing the plateau. The hills erupted with flashes as their venom-guns went into action and the Zarbi poured down to meet the invaders. The Menoptera crouched and fired at the oncoming hordes – but it was as if their electron combat-guns were harmless toys. Realizing this, some of the Menoptera threw their guns aside and backed for the shelter of the hills and rocks around the plateau. They ran and fell as the deadly murderous stings spat and smoked on their crumpled bodies. Others stood their ground and launched themselves barehanded with suicidal courage at the oncoming Zarbi.

Now the fighting was all about them. One Zarbi on a near-by crest paused and directed the sting of its creature into the sky. A Menoptera, flying in to land, crumpled suddenly and fell out of space like a plummet.

'Look out!'

It was Hlynia who screamed the warning to Barbara and the others. A Zarbi had appeared on the crest of the rocks overlooking their own shelter and now with a gesture of its claw it summoned its sting grub.

They all saw the danger, and unarmed as they were, there was nothing for it but to turn and run. Alone, the Menoptera officer, Hilio, who had dropped to the ground from the crag and joined them, faced the sting-gun and levelled his own weapon. It spat harmlessly. He fired again, and again.

The ground erupted around him as the sting creature poised its snout and answered with a staccato flashing.

'It's useless!' Hrostar yelled. He threw himself on Hilio and dragged him away. They turned and ran, heading around a corner of the rock and into a defile with the Zarbi and its sting grub slithering after them.

As they ran Barbara halted and stared ahead of them in dismay. She turned despairingly to the others as they panted towards her – Hlynia, Prapillus, Hrostar and Hilio. She pointed.

'No exit!'

The others halted. Ahead of them rose sheer rock face.

'We've run into a dead end!'

'Are there no crevices leading off?'

Barbara turned and ran towards the rock face, casting about desperately for an escape. There was none. They were hemmed in by rock on all sides.

'No . . .!'

There was a scuttling behind them. First the venom-gun slithered malignantly into sight round the corner of the closed defile – and then its Zarbi master.

The sting grub poised, levelled its snout, aiming it at the group now huddled and backing hopelessly against the sheer rock wall.

The Zarbi, its great eyes glaring, raised a foreclaw, then brought it down.

The sting-gun fired.

CHAPTER FIVE

Invasion

As the murderous sting fired, the cornered party scattered wildly. The first flash hit the sheer rock face as Barbara sidled along it.

The wall smouldered – and moved.

Barbara wheeled, staring.

A great crack appeared in the rock – and it sprang apart, like the opening wings of a giant Menoptera, revealing a cavern inside. Barbara shrieked and pointed as the sting-gun flashed again and the ground beneath her feet burned and smoked.

'Look – in here!'

The others turned, gaping, and plunged desperately through the opening. They tumbled inside the cavern as the venom-gun spat again and a huge chip of rock above Hrostar's head broke off, smouldering, and fell.

Then, with a mighty grinding, the slabs of rock clashed down behind them.

Barbara and her Menoptera companions lay sprawled on the floor, safe for the moment, shielded by a great wall of rock, breathing heavily and not daring to question the great miracle which had spared them.

As they got their breath back they began to look around them. Hlynia was the first to recover.

Her eyes opened wide as she took in the sight which greeted her.

She pointed.

'Look . . .!' Hlynia breathed.

The web indicator on the great Zarbi control panel glowed and flashed as its lights reported the story of the ambush and the rout of the invading Menoptera.

The speakers below it hummed and buzzed triumphantly with the news of the Zarbi victory.

During all this Doctor Who and Vicki stood motionless against the wall as if carved out of stone, staring unseeingly ahead, their faces blank.

In their furious excitement and intentness on the battle the Zarbi appeared to have forgotten their earth captives.

Vicki was the first to come 'alive'. She stole a quick sidelong glance at the creatures chirruping and bustling around the control panel – and then she looked at the Doctor.

She reached out furtively, snatched the necklet from around the Doctor's throat, and dropped it hastily as if it were hot.

Doctor Whoblinked and awoke to an awareness of his surroundings. Vicki quietly put a hand on his arm and motioned him with a finger to silence.

Doctor Who stared at the necklet still encircling the girl.

'Vicki – you're still wearing the . . .!' he whispered.

She smiled, calmly removed her own necklet, and offered it to him.

She whispered back, 'It's the one you treated. I slipped it in the Zarbi's way when I saw what they were going to do. You succeeded, Doctor – it doesn't work any more . . .!'

Doctor Who took the necklet and examined it carefully, keeping an eye on the Zarbi. He stared at the smiling Vicki.

She said, 'When they directed us to the wall, I just . . . walked there. I shammed!'

'My dear child . . .!'

'Oh!' Vicki shrugged lightly, rather pleased with herself. 'It was nothing, really . . .'

'Nonsense! You have a very sharp brain! Now we must take advantage of . . . this discovery . . .!'

The Doctor rubbed his chin and swivelled his head carefully to stare towards the Zarbi. Again he pondered the necklet.

'Hmm . . . if it no longer works on us, it seems I have managed to reverse the . . . force field . . . well, well . . .!'

'Careful – look out!' Vicki breathed.

The activity at the control panel was slackening. The speaker, having hummed a final set of instructions, shut off the big light in the centre of the web indicator faded and blanked out. The Zarbi manning the control panel relaxed. One of them turned, looked towards the Doctor and Vicki, got up, and marched towards them.

Vicki and Doctor Who stiffened to attention, staring before them, pretending to be still in a trance.

The Zarbi passed them with only a brief flash of its glowing eyes and headed for one of the exits. It vanished down a tunnel.

Another Zarbi moved away from the control panel and crouched sleepily, leaving a single companion manning the controls. Doctor Who relaxed faintly. He took the bracelet he had treated and slipped it on his own neck. He kicked the other necklet in front of Vicki and nodded at it. Out of the corner of his mouth he whispered, 'Now, child – this is what I want you to do . . .'

As he whispered to Vicki the Zarbi at the control panel turned its head slightly. Then it rose at a sound from Vicki.

The girl was 'awake'. She was staring around her bewildered.

'What's happened . . .?' She called. 'Where . . . am I . . .?'

The Zarbi stared and saw the necklet had apparently fallen from her and was lying at her feet. It chirruped and scuttled across to her from the panel. Its claw reached to pick up the necklet and replace it on the dazed girl. As it stopped Doctor Who moved swiftly. He whipped the treated gold circle from his own throat and thrust it at the Zarbi's thin neck, between the evil head and the sleek body.

The Zarbi stiffened, reared. Doctor Who tensed against the expected blow. The Zarbi remained staring at Doctor Who.

Suddenly it grew stiff, motionless. Vicki shot a questioning, anxious look sidelong at the Doctor. He watched the Zarbi. He raised a hand – and directed it.

Obediently the Zarbi turned as he pointed.

Vicki smothered a wild yell of excitement. Doctor Who was beaming now, and chuckling.

'Splendid ... splendid ...!'

'But ... what can we do now?'

'Eh?' Doctor Who pondered that slyly. Slowly his face lit with mischief – and hope.

'Well – I think we should get our friend to take us out of here, don't you think? It's essential that we contact these Menoptera, my dear ...'

Vicki flashed an anxious look at the other Zarbi guard still in the control room, resting itself, its head turned away. She looked towards the tunnel exits.

'But ... they won't let us out of here just like that ...!'

Doctor Who was wagging his head over that problem.

'I don't know ...' he mused. 'Now – if the other creatures think that *we* are the ones being directed – to this slave colony the Voice spoke of, for instance – they *might*, mightn't they? Mm ...?'

'I ... suppose so ...' Vicki said uncertainly.

Doctor Who seized her arm reassuringly. 'Come along then – let's try it ...!'

He turned and pointed at the Zarbi, then towards the nearest doorway to a tunnel.

Dully, the Zarbi responded. It walked on its ungainly hind legs towards the tunnel.

There Doctor Who stopped it with a commanding finger. He placed himself and Vicki in front of the Zarbi. Then he turned and beckoned the Zarbi to follow.

As they entered the tunnel a Zarbi guard emerged from the far end and came scuttling along towards them. Doctor Who and Vicki walked steadily towards it, their faces blank, apparently unseeing, the creature under their control shuffling along behind them.

The oncoming guard paused, glaring curiously – and then passed on.

Only when it had passed did Vicki venture a look around them.

'I expected to see more of these Zarbi creatures about than this, Doctor.'

'Mm – they must have been sent to the plateau ... to meet this spearhead ... Be careful now – I'm afraid we've still a long way to go ...'

They walked warily on down the tunnel.

Barbara was staring about her in wonderment. So were her Menoptera friends – Hrostar, Prapillus, Hlynia and Hilio.

'It's ... a temple,' Hlynia breathed.

'An ancient Menoptera temple,' Prapillus murmured. 'It must be fifty generations old.'

Hrostar pointed at the walls. 'It was of such things that our great civilization was made.'

Their voices had a strange echoing quality. The great sheer walls were carved with immense designs of Menoptera wings, and still – though crumbling and decayed – brilliantly coloured. Gold and coppery markings, some of them turned to a luminous green with age, shone down among the ochres, the reds and sky-blues of the vivid wing patterns.

They saw that the rock walls which had opened to let them in and then closed behind them were shaped and carved too, into the pattern of a massive pair of wings.

Prapillus, the wise old scholar among them, was entranced. 'One of our temples of light,' he whispered. 'I knew they existed. The legends about them have been handed down. But I thought they were lost forever ...'

Hlynia turned to her father. 'There are *others*?'

Prapillus nodded. 'According to the stories – scattered in the craters and the plateaux of Vortis ... slowly crumbling away, their locations long since forgotten as our ancestors sank into slavery ...'

Barbara and Hrostar were leaning against the great winged walls, now folded down, closed.

'It sounds as if they've gone ... given up,' Barbara said.

Hrostar faced their party. 'One of us must explore.'

Prapillus shook his head. 'No, Hrostar, not yet. The Zarbi are almost certain to mount guards. We must wait. Perhaps ... find another way out.' The old Menoptera looked around him.

Hrostar stared up at the brilliant walls. 'The Light God was kind to us today. It is a good omen.'

'Is it?' Barbara challenged him. 'From what I saw of the battle – the spearhead was wiped out!'

The spearhead officer Hilio drew himself up, proud and confident. 'All is not lost – the main invasion force will soon arrive. Then we will triumph!'

'But they were relying on your spearhead, weren't they, Hilio?' Barbara asked.

'It was only . . . a . . . a setback. But we will not be stopped by the Zarbi! After all these years of planning, it is now or never. Nothing will stop us! Even if our electron-guns proved, er, disappointing in battle against the Zarbi, we shall rely on our numbers, our . . . courage!'

'It is fine to make patriotic speeches, Hilio,' the old Menoptera Prapillus said coldly. 'But they will not free Vortis for us!'

'You must face it,' Barbara urged him. 'Both your scouting party and your spearhead failed! The Zarbi routed them! The same will happen to your main force – unless you change your plans. You *must* think of a new way to outwit these creatures – this intelligence which controls them.'

'Very well!' Hrostar wheeled and faced Barbara. 'How can we establish a landing point for our forces? Tell me that!'

Barbara shook her head. 'We couldn't! But . . . perhaps we could do something else – just as effective.'

Hilio pointed a scornful finger at Barbara. 'Should we listen to a stranger? Let the invasion go on! Some of us will get through! We must!'

Prapillus held up his hand. 'Hilio – surely this disaster has taught you something good.'

'Good?' Hilio exploded.

Prapillus nodded. 'We Menoptera are blessed with the power of flight. It has made us god-like in our confidence – that we can rise above any difficulty, instead of solving it. It has made you blind! But we slaves are not blind. When we had our wings clipped or taken from us, we were forced to use our brains, to think! For that lesson we must *thank* the Zarbi!'

He turned towards Barbara. 'And we can learn much from this earth girl. Sheer courage alone is not enough to win us victory. We must be ready to change tactics, plan, scheme, *outwit* . . .!'

Hilio folded his arms. 'Very well,' he said sarcastically. 'Let us listen to this girl – and her brilliant ideas.'

There was a pause. All eyes were on Barbara.

She said uncertainly, 'Well . . . if your spearhead *had* been successful, what would you have then done?'

'If we had met no resistance,' Hilio answered curtly, 'We would have proceeded to the centre of the great web growing over Vortis – and destroyed whatever it is that controls the Zarbi!'

'How?'

Hilio paused. He looked at them, hesitated, then drew out a small instrument the size of a pistol from inside his brilliant combat jacket. It had a short, thick snout, but instead of a target sight, it was equipped with a tiny, saucer-shaped mirror with an electrode projecting from its centre. At the trigger end the barrel was wound thickly with fine wires, like an armature, and studded with a circle of brilliantly coloured tubes the size of transistor valves. A short tension-sprung lever switch took the place of a trigger.

Hilio held the weapon carefully before him.

'With this,' he said.

'What is it?' Prapillus asked, his bright old eyes alight with interest.

'A whole generation of our scientists have been working to produce it. It was called Project V-W-D. It is designed for one use – against the Intelligence which controls the Zarbi. You would understand it better if I called it by the name our invasion command has given it. They know it as . . . the Web Destructor.'

Prapillus stretched forward his hand and reluctantly Hilio allowed him to handle the instrument. The old Menoptera examined it keenly, his eyes roving over the armature with its cluster of brilliant tubes and the tiny glittering dish-shaped sight.

'... A ... living cell destructor ...?' Prapillus ventured, musing. 'Correct ...?'

Hilio nodded. 'That web and the living thing behind it is an organic matter that *grows* – and spreads its evil around Vortis. This destructor will reverse the process ... the cells will mutate, grow inwards – and the being will be destroyed ...'

Prapillus finished admiring the Web Destructor and restored it to Hilio. He wagged his head doubtfully.

'It is precious little use to you, though, while the Zarbi stand in your way. Your ordinary electron-guns proved useless against them.'

Hilio hung his head and admitted that. 'We must expect setbacks. We are prepared for massive casualties.'

Barbara shook her head. 'That is not the way!' she said. 'It is folly to waste countless lives! The thing is to get *behind* this creature's shield – The Zarbi – and strike at its heart. I agree with Hilio about one thing ...'

'Yes ...?' Prapillus prompted her.

'The key to all this is to attack the centre – the Intelligence behind it. What I do not agree about is that we should try to reach it by overcoming the Zarbi in open battle.'

'When our invasion force lands ...' Hilio began to say ...

Barbara rounded on him. 'Force is not the answer! You have seen what happened on the plateau! Has that taught you *nothing*? It could mean suicide for your whole army.'

'She is right,' Prapillus said. He tapped his head. 'We must attack the centre. But to get to it – we must *think*, use ... guile ...!'

The pigmy-like underground kinsmen of the Menoptera now crowded respectfully around Vrestin and the earth man Ian, listening spellbound to their story and the plan they unfolded for their future.

It was as though Vrestin's glowing words had opened up new vistas for them. He told them of their rich heritage, of what history had told of the true civilization on Vortis, how rich and splendid it had been.

It was this civilization that the rescuing Menoptera were returning to restore.

But the way would be hard and fraught with danger, Vrestin and Ian had warned them.

Now they crowded about the two men, pointing out the tunnels they had dug with their curious whorl-shaped spears. Their skill with these implements was impressive. Not only had they adapted them for their defence, but they burrowed and dug through the ground with incredible speed, turning them around rock and dislodging solid veins of silica with tremendous dexterity. They used the natural underground fissures and chasms they came upon, too, to join the complex of tunnels which made up their underground home.

Now they shouldered their spears and listened afresh as Ian and Vrestin unfolded a plan to reach and bore into the very heart of the planet's great enemy – the being whose vibrations controlled the hated Zarbi and whose web crawled and tightened its evil grip on Vortis.

Ian was drawing a design on the floor of the chamber in which they sat.

'We'll make our way underground, through your tunnels, digging where we have to – until we're underneath the web.'

Vrestin pointed. 'Then upwards, into its soft under-belly.'

Hetra straightened. He looked at his comrades, their slitted eyes now glowing with excitement and hope.

'Very well,' Hetra quavered. '*You* know what faces us. We can only agree.'

There was a mutter of assent.

Hetra beckoned to his deputy, Nemini. 'It will be better if Nemini leads – there are many dangers in the tunnels.'

Ian looked as Nemini approached. 'Very well. Tell him we'll have to hurry. Time is short.'

Nemini paused at that, and looked at Ian. 'Don't worry about my speed. You just worry about keeping up with me!'

He shouldered his spear and marched ahead. Hetra signalled to the others. 'Forward!' Vrestin watched his dwarfish Menoptera kinsmen march after Nemini. He turned a doubtful face to Ian.

'I wonder how much we can count on them . . .' he said.

'Do we have a choice?'

'They are all right down here, Ian – but what when we strike upward? Their fears of the surface may prove too strong.'

'Let's worry about that when it happens. Come on!'

They moved off after the pigmy diggers. The leader Nemini paused as they emerged from a tunnel into a natural underground cave, bristling like a forest, with stalagmites and stalactites, reaching from floor and roof. Nemini swung his coiled tool, snapping off enough of the sharp spars to clear a way for them, and led on.

As Ian followed he saw cracks in the wall of the caves – and through these seeped wreaths of misty smoke. He nudged Vrestin and pointed, frowning. A wisp of the fumes stung his nostrils. He coughed and they plunged on.

Doctor Who and Vicki, still stepping ahead of the Zarbi, turned into a new tunnel and stopped. In front of them a webbed gate hung down and blocked the exit. Beside it hovered a Zarbi guard. The Doctor turned, stared at the Zarbi standing docilely under his control. He reached out, touched the necklet encircling its scraggy throat and stared into its dull eyes meaningly. Then he pointed towards the guarded web-gate and walked on stiffly, as though under the creature's control.

He and Vicki dared do nothing but gaze straight ahead of them as they came up to the gate. Out of the corner of their eyes they flashed a brief glance at the guard who now reared questioningly, and chirruped.

It was answered by a slow, muted chirrup from the slow-moving creature behind them.

The guard turned its glaring eyes on the Doctor. Then abruptly it touched a lever in the tunnel wall.

The webbed gate rose high in the air – and beyond them stretched the scarred, crag-dotted landscape of Vortis.

Doctor Who took a deep breath and stepped out. Vicki followed. They walked slowly, stiffly on, not daring now to look behind them. They listened intently but heard no sound of alarm. Only when they had reached a rise and the shelter of a line of rocks did they risk a pause, and turned. The Zarbi shuffled along obediently in their wake.

'How will we find the plateau?' Vicki asked.

Doctor Who pointed. 'Simple,' he said. 'Zarbi tracks. Those who left the web were surely headed that way. We simply follow. This way, my dear.'

He turned and gestured to the Zarbi. Vicki smiled. 'I'm getting quite fond of Zombo,' she said.

'Of *whom*?'

'That's what I call him. When they behave so tamely, they're rather ... cute, don't you think?'

'No, I do *not*! I find them revolting! I hope you've got no idea of making a pet of him!'

'Well ...'

'We're not taking him aboard *Tardis*, mind! Now hurry, child.'

Vicki smiled at the Doctor's anxiety and crooked a finger at the Zarbi as it followed them dazedly down a slope.

Even the pigmy diggers were coughing now as they ploughed onward through the tunnel-like caves and the mist seeping from the fissures in the walls thickened.

'Air's getting terrible,' Ian muttered.

'Hurry,' Vrestin urged, 'don't let them get too far ahead of us.'

Even Nemini and Hetra, leading the column, had to pause, coughing.

'The gas is getting thicker,' Nemini said.

Hetra looked about them. 'Is there no other way forward?'

Nemini shook his head. 'We'll have to cut our way through the wall – and hope we can find an adjoining tunnel that is clear.'

Ian and Vrestin stumbled into sight. They had caught up with the pigmy leaders.

'What's wrong?'

'Delay,' Hetra replied. 'We shall have to dig.'

'We could track back,' Nemini offered, 'and pick up another route . . .'

Ian looked around at the walls and the ceiling.

'I don't like the idea of digging here. Look at those cracks. Is it . . . safe?'

'Ian!' Vrestin shouted, beckoning from farther back in the tunnel. Ian turned and jumped towards Vrestin, who held up a hand, listening, head cocked towards the rear.

They heard a rumbling behind them. It rose in volume. The ceiling above them split and opened. Ian wrenched at Vrestin's arm, dragged him clear, and together they leaped for safety as, with a great tearing and grinding of rock, the roof where they had been standing fell in. Silica rock and glassy earth tumbled and roared, deafening them and sending up great choking eddies of dust.

When it settled and all was silent again they saw the gas swirling in through a host of cracks which the fall had opened in the wall. Ian stared.

'We're cut off! Blocked on all sides! It'll take hours to clear!'

Hetra raised a hand urgently. 'Nemini – we'll have to go on. Start the men digging through!'

The pigmy diggers glared at the task ahead of them, at the cracks in the walls around through which the noxious mist was seeping thickly now. They picked up their spiral spears and began attacking the rock face ahead of them. Vrestin was coughing and choking.

'Can . . . hardly breathe . . .!' he gasped.

'There's no outlet for these gases now!' Ian muttered. He turned as one of their diggers, coughing and retching, staggered and crumpled in a heap on the floor.

Ian bent and grabbed the digger's tool and attacked the wall furiously.

'Dig! Dig like mad! Or we'll all suffocate!'

The frail Hetra was the next to collapse as the thick-swirling fumes billowed about them. Ian and Vrestin both had tools now and were joining the others hacking furiously at the walls in their frenzied efforts to tear a way out of the trap.

Through the thick smoke he saw the workers' leader Nemini clutch at his throat and fall, then the tiny digger next to Ian sank to the floor. Still Ian drove furiously on, heedless of those who were choking and sinking about him, holding his own breath as long as he could. But the effort was making him gasp – and take in great gulps of the fumes, denser now than the thickest London fog.

'Are you all right, Vrestin?'

'A faint muffled call answered him. 'All . . . right . . . but everybody else . . . out . . .'

Ian attacked the wall like a man demented. He felt his strength ebbing. He had to pause, wrapped a handkerchief around his mouth, tried breathing through it. He picked up the tool and again slogged at the wall, his strokes becoming more feeble and aimless. He coughed and retched. He felt a dizziness now, and his knees were buckling.

He could hardly see any more. It was no use. They were all doomed, he thought dimly, to be gassed to death in this tomb of a place.

His eyes began to close and he sank to his knees.

A large web had been scratched in the floor of the temple and Barbara pondered it wearily.

They had been arguing – for hours it seemed – about the best way to reach the centre. It was the newcomer Hilio who had proved the biggest stumbling block to any really novel plan. Try as he might to agree, the Menoptera officer could not cast off his lofty confidence in attacking openly – in spite of the grim lesson his ill-fated spearhead had just been given.

Barbara stared at the map and said again, 'I still think that the best idea is to create a mock attack on one of the web openings, while one of us tries to reach the centre from the opposite side . . .'

'It will fail!' Hilio declared. 'Even if it drew most of the

defences, it would only need one sting grub to stop anybody penetrating in from the other side!'

'Still,' Prapillus murmured, 'with only five of us, it does seem the best strategy . . .'

'I agree,' Hrostar said, 'It's still terribly risky, but I can see no sensible alternative.'

Hilio stood up. 'Very well! I shall go in alone from the other side!'

Hrostar looked at Hilio scornfully. 'You? When you don't even believe in its success?'

Hilio glared back, opened his mouth to retort, and Barbara interrupted hastily. 'Please . . . please – we can decide who goes by drawing lots.'

'No!' Hrostar insisted. He looked around at them. 'Two women . . . an old man . . . and an unbeliever – I am the natural choice!'

Barbara looked at him and smiled. The proud Hrostar had drawn himself up and spread his magnificent wings.

'You'll also be the most easily spotted,' she reminded him gently.

'Shh!' Hlynia commanded. She was standing at the winged rock door, listening intently. 'Quiet, there's somebody outside!'

They all stood stock-still. From the other side of the rock they heard it clearly now – a faint scratching.

'Not very loud,' Barbara said.

'Open the door – just a crack,' Prapillus suggested.

'No!' Hilio exclaimed. 'It must be the Zarbi!'

'Then we'll see – won't we,' Prapillus retorted. 'Carefully, Hrostar. The rock is counterbalanced, look. Be ready to slam it shut instantly if . . .'

They waited as Hrostar applied his weight to the winged door of rock. It swung back suddenly several feet – and they recoiled. A Zarbi stood there, reared, and came scuttling in. Hilio dived for the electron-gun. The others scattered and grabbed around them for rocks, spars, any weapon. Hrostar lunged to close the door aperture behind the lone Zarbi.

'Wait!' Barbara yelled. 'Look – friends!'

The Zarbi had come to a halt and simply stood there motionless and peaceful. Behind it, poised at the entrance, stood the slight, frock-coated figure of – Doctor Who! Vicki stood clinging to the doctor, staring at them.

'Hello?' the Doctor called cheerfully. 'Any body at home? Please – don't attack him! He's harmless . . .'

Barbara rushed out to greet the Doctor. He and Vicki saw her and his kindly face wrinkled into an amazed beam of delight. Vicki shrieked excitedly, 'Barbara! It's Barbara!'

'My dear girl,' the Doctor stammered, 'What an extremely pleasant surprise!'

'Doctor . . . Vicki!' Barbara gasped, unable to express her joy and relief.

They hugged each other. Doctor Who looked about him inquiringly.

'Is, um, Chesterton not with you?'

Barbara stared back, her joy fading.

'No . . . no! What . . . has happened to him . . .?'

They all looked at each other, troubled, wondering.

All was silent now in the underground tunnel. The figures of the pigmy-menoptera diggers, of Ian and Vrestin, were strewn about the floor like so many corpses.

One of the figures stirred weakly. It was Ian. He dragged himself to his knees and looked hazily about. He remembered, and sniffed.

The poisonous mist had thinned. The air was almost clear. He reached out a hand to touch the body of Vrestin, and stirred him. Vrestin groaned and moved. The Menoptera's eyes fluttered open. He sat up with difficulty on one elbow and stared.

'The gas – it's gone!'

Ian nodded. On the other side of them Nemini was waking. The dwarf Menoptera peered dimly at the tunnel walls which enclosed them, and pointed. A large fissure showed.

'Air currents,' Nemini muttered, and coughed. 'Pressures in these tunnels rise and fall without warning. They cause

rock falls . . . they press in fumes . . . then . . . suck them out, just as quickly.'

Ian got up. 'We're in luck.'

'Indeed,' Vrestin muttered. Hetra was reviving. He called weakly to the others, 'We must continue our journey before it returns. Nemini . . .! Rouse as many of our diggers as you can . . .'

Nemini nodded and went among his workers, shaking them awake. Two of them did not respond. They remained huddled where they were, and Nemini halted, looking down.

'Can we try reviving them?' Ian asked.

Nemini shook his head. 'The gases thinned too late – for them,' he said, and turned away towards the rock face. He raised a spear probe and tapped at the wall. Nemini nodded at Ian.

'Here . . . the wall is thinner! Stand back.'

Ian moved back to allow Nemini room. The stocky little Menoptera swung his digger and struck at the wall. A crack opened suddenly – and as it did so, fumes, then liquid spurted through. Nemini gave a yell and staggered back.

'A leak – from the surface! Get back!'

'The acid pools!' Ian yelled. 'Nemini, come away!'

But Nemini stood his ground. Ian wheeled to Hetra. 'Order him back!'

Hetra shook his head. 'Someone must block that gap! Otherwise we shall all die!'

Ian made to leap forward, but Hetra raised a hand and two pigmy diggers grabbed at him and pulled him back. Ian stared in fascinated horror as Nemini, snatching up handfuls of rock and gritting his teeth against the agonizing pain of the liquid that spurted through, splattering and drenching him, frantically worked to block the gap.

'He doesn't stand a chance!'

Hetra watched stonily, his lined old face drawn and tense. He shrugged.

'It is a danger that is always with us,' he said simply. He rounded on the other workers. 'Try the other wall – quickly!'

Somehow the reeling Nemini had succeeded in packing the seeping crack with loose rock and now he staggered back, groaning and weaving to and fro in agony. Ian started forward to help him but as he did so the short figure of the workers' leader crumpled to the floor. Nemini stretched out and immediately stiffened.

Ian reached down to touch the dead pigmy Menoptera and halted in horrified amazement. The eyes were already sightless. The body, where his hand touched it, was brittle and crumbly, as though mummified. He remembered the hollow body his foot had crunched into when he and the Doctor had first emerged from *Tardis* to explore this planet.

It had happened in a matter of moments.

A call came from Vrestin, leading the other workers in an attack on another part of the cave wall.

'Ian – we're through!'

Hetra touched Ian's arm gently. 'Come . . .!'

Ian got to his feet. There was nothing anybody could do for Nemini now. Ian looked backward at the body as he walked and stumbled over rock.

'Coming . . .' he muttered.

Doctor Who stood in the centre of the ancient temple, looking down thoughtfully upon the map and the plan of Vortis that the others had drawn.

Vicki had directed the harmless Zarbi into a corner. Hlynia stood at the door, waiting and listening, on guard, while the three Menoptera men stood respectfully back, awaiting the Doctor's verdict.

Doctor Who raised his head.

'M'yes . . . yes . . . very detailed sketch . . . Excellent . . .'

'Do we have a chance, Doctor?' Barbara asked.

Doctor Who considered that. 'I think so, my dear.' He turned to the Menoptera Officer, Hilio. 'Tell me, Captain – what *is* at the centre of this web, mm? Do *you* know?'

Hilio shook his head and turned the question to Prapillûs. The old Menoptera came forward.

'Nobody here knows for certain – an alien Intelligence, definitely . . . but its shape, or form . . .?'

Prapillus shrugged.

'But if it arrived here,' Barbara said, 'from another planet – then surely *somebody* must have seen it!'

Prapillus shook his hoary head. 'Such research as I have been able to make shows that its presence was only noticed when it was already gaining power, controlling the Zarbi . . . spreading its web . . . only then did they know that something had risen into being here . . . our people were only interested in a peaceful life. They were probably quite unaware of it for years . . .'

'Yes, yes – quite understandable. But – Prapillus, did your studies show where this . . . this *force* it possesses is drawn from . . .?'

Prapillus hunched his frail shoulders. 'The answer may be found in one fact perhaps,' he said simply.

'What is that?'

Prapillus eyed Doctor Who and replied slowly.

'The centre of the web rests on the magnetic pole of this planet,' he said.

Doctor Who's face cleared suddenly and he stared.

'Of course! Of course! It is drawing on – using – the actual power of the *Planet Vortis*!'

'It would explain, would it not, these new satellites that have appeared on the sky, Doctor? They too could have been pulled here by this . . . power . . .!'

Doctor Who was wagging his head. 'Tch-tch – I should have realized that! Yes – the same force drew and held *Tardis* here! Well, well . . .!'

He stroked his chin and moved away to digest and ponder this new light on the Intelligence behind the web. Barbara hesitated to interrupt his reverie. Finally she ventured, 'Doctor – are you going to go ahead with the plan?'

'Eh? Mmm? Oh . . . yes, my dear, er – with a slight variation . . . Yes!'

'A change?' Hrostar asked. 'What?'

Doctor Who turned and faced them. 'You can carry out

the mock attack as planned – your job, Barbara. We'll agree a time.'

Barbara nodded. Hilio picked up the Destructor. 'And this?'

Doctor Who reached out a hand. 'I'll take that, if I may, Vicki and I will return to Zarbi Headquarters.'

Hrostar nodded at the Web Destructor. 'Can you smuggle *that* past the Zarbi?'

'I don't see why not,' the Doctor said calmly. 'I came out with this . . .'

And he pulled out an electron-gun from under his old-fashioned frock-coat.

'An electron-gun – useless,' Hrostar growled.

'So I discovered . . . when I examined it,' the Doctor murmured. 'And for a good reason.'

'Oh?'

'I suspect,' Doctor Who explained, 'that the reason it could not hit its target was that the Zarbi bodies deflected its aim. Repelled it – magnetically . . . in some way . . .'

'Then the Web Destructor is probably just as useless!' Hrostar maintained.

Doctor Who shrugged at that. 'Perhaps there's a way . . .' he murmured, half to himself. He brightened cheerfully. 'Well, we shall have to take that chance! Eh? To me, the design of this Destructor appears far more promising. Your men of science seem to have given it far more thought . . .'

He smiled at them, turned away to go, halted, and patted the Destructor.

He said dryly, 'In any case, we have no choice . . .'

A pause. The Menoptera eyed each other uncertainly.

'Any questions?' Doctor Who murmured.

'May we get it clear, Doctor?' Barbara asked. 'You're going to return to the Headquarters. Once you are inside, we attack, draw the Zarbi – leaving you to make for the centre of the . . . web . . .'

Doctor Who beamed on her. 'Excellent – full marks, for a clear, simple summary.' He turned. 'Vicki, my child . . .?'

Glumly Vicki came forward. She hung her head in order

not to show her dislike for going back to the evil web –
among the Zarbi. Doctor Who saw it and understood. He
patted her gently.

'Don't worry, my dear. Um ... in fact ... I don't parti-
cularly want to go back there either.'

Vicki mustered a smile for him. 'It's all right. After all, we
do stand the best chance. Anyway – the *Tardis* is still there ...'

'Good girl, good girl.'

A call from Prapillus checked them.

'Doctor ...?'

Doctor Who crossed to join Prapillus. 'Yes – what is it?' he
asked, testily.

Prapillus pointed at the captive Zarbi. 'I, er, wondered if
we could borrow this creature. He will be very useful in our
attack.'

Doctor Who stiffened. 'You think so?' he sniffed icily. 'And
how, pray, do we get back into the Headquarters without it?'

Prapillus smiled calmly. 'I'm sure your brains are equal to
that. Besides, if a lifetime of slavery has robbed me of a
scientific career – at least *I* have made a study of the Zarbi
... and could use him better.'

Doctor Who drew himself up in thunderous outrage.

'Oh, really! Better than I, Mmm? And who managed to
gain control of it? Eh?'

'That may be. But I have the experience, I am an old
man ...'

'And what do you think I am – sweet sixteen?' Doctor
Who roared. 'How old *are* you?'

Barbara heard the dispute and moved smoothly towards
the two old men. 'Doctor ... Prapillus – is something
wrong?'

Doctor Who turned brusquely away. 'Oh, nothing, my
dear ... nothing ...'

'A small matter, a small matter,' Prapillus muttered and
glared at the Doctor's back.

Doctor Who simmered down, relented. 'Prapillus made
the brilliant suggestion that he took this creature with your
party ... that's all ...' he said.

'. . . and I was congratulating the Doctor on his achievements over the Zarbi,' Prapillus said, gently, swallowing hard and mustering a polite smile for the Doctor.

'Oh – for a minute it sounded like a row . . .!'

'Bless my soul,' Doctor Who exclaimed, 'Never . . .!'

Prapillus wagged his head reprovingly at Barbara. 'Really, nothing could be farther from the—'

'I should have thought you'd have known me better than that, my dear,' Doctor Who added. He gave his rival Prapillus a wintry smile. 'Young people have very little respect, Prapillus. You must forgive her.'

'Come, Vicki,' Doctor Who called. He raised a commanding hand at the Zarbi.

'Here, you – what did you call him, child? . . . Zombo . . .!'

The Zarbi scuttled obediently forward. The Doctor thought a moment and turned to Prapillus.

'There is a way in which this creature may . . . serve us both . . .' he mused.

'How, Doctor?'

'. . . supposing I were to use the Zarbi to get me back to the centre . . . and then – I sent him back to you . . .?'

Prapillus beamed delightedly. 'Capital, my dear Doctor . . . a truly splendid thought . . .!'

Doctor Who bowed. 'Coming from a thinker like yourself, that is a compliment indeed.'

Doctor Who paused for a last look at Barbara and the Menoptera, gathered to watch them go.

'When we meet again,' he said quietly, 'let us hope this evil that rules on Vortis will be ended forever.'

The Doctor turned and strode away, with Vicki holding his hand.

Hrostar watched them go gloomily.

'*If* we ever meet again . . .' he said, and stared out at the gloomy Vortis landscape as the rock wings parted to let them through.

Ian, Vrestin and the pigmy-menoptera leaders had now broken clear through into another tunnel and were hurrying

along, stumbling over rock and around the bristling stalagmites in the direction pointed out by the aged Hetra.

As they forged ahead they became aware of a pulsing
sound which seemed to come from the very rock itself above
their heads. It was like a faint, steady heartbeat. Ian heard it
and paused, clutching at Vrestin's arm. They went on slowly
now – and then the frail land of Hetra stayed them with a
warning gesture.

They listened. Hetra stared around above him, head
cocked.

He turned to Ian and Vrestin – and nodded.

'The web – it is right above us now.'

He turned and signalled to his diggers. They came running
forward, looking up – a little awed.

Ian braced himself. He pointed to the roof of the tunnel.

'We go up – there!' he announced.

The stocky diggers hesitated a little, then mustered their
courage and sprang forward. As agilely as monkeys they
swarmed up the stalagmites till their curled spears were
within reach of the roof.

They began attacking it, weaving aside as the rock they
levered came crashing down to the cave floor. The diggers
exchanged worried glances among each other as they
hesitated and dug farther upward.

Ian noted their fear. He exchanged a look with Vrestin.

'I . . . hope they will not let us down,' he muttered, eyeing
the diggers anxiously.

Cautiously, Barbara led her Menoptera companions in the
wake of the distant figures of Doctor Who, Vicki and the
obedient Zarbi. She halted them and they sheltered in
the shadow of a crag.

Doctor Who had reached an opening in the great web
which now reared ahead, its light wheeling and flashing over
the landscape and outlining the crag under which they stood.

'The web is opening – they're going in!' she whispered.

'We'll wait on your word . . . when to attack,' Prapillus
murmured.

Barbara nodded, watching. 'Thank you. We'll wait – make sure the Doctor has got back to the Control Section . . .'

The Guard let the Doctor and Vicki into the entrance tunnel, together with the Zarbi, without challenge or hindrance.

Once inside the web tunnel Doctor Who halted and turned. He gestured commandingly to the Zarbi and pointed.

The creature stopped, hesitated. Doctor Who glared, willing it to understand him and obey. He pointed again.

The Zarbi wheeled and scuttled back towards the entrance through which they had come. The Zarbi guarding the outer door paused, staring, then raised the webbed barrier and let its comrade through – watching it lurch away across the landscape.

Doctor Who and Vicki saw it go. The Doctor rubbed his hands.

'Excellent – *excellent!* . . . doing exactly as it's told! Let's hope that old . . . er, let's hope Prapillus makes good use of him. Come, child . . .!'

The Doctor took Vicki's arm and headed down the corridor in the direction of the control room.

As they made their way tortuously down tunnel after tunnel leading inward, they were aware of furious activity, somewhere ahead of them.

The whole air throbbed and even from a distance they could hear the agitated chirruping. The noise of it burst upon them afresh as they rounded a corner and saw, ahead of them, the figures in the control room at the end of the corridor.

Vicki clung to Doctor Who, trembling all over now, knowing that something was wrong.

'I'm . . . I'm . . . frightened. Please, Doctor, can we—?'

Doctor Who laid a calm hand on her arm. He smiled and marched purposefully forward. As they entered the control room, assuming a trance-like look and pretending to step like sleepwalkers, the agitated figures at the control panel wheeled and saw them.

A furious burst of chirruping rose and three of the Zarbi

whirled and came scuttling menacingly towards them, rearing, their forelegs waving, their eyes glaring murderously.

Vicki covered her mouth to stifle a scream of fear and dismay.

'Doctor – they've missed us! Now the plan will never work . . .!'

CHAPTER SIX

Centre of Terror

The Zarbi pounced on Doctor Who and Vicki and jostled them forward towards the centre of the room.

The Doctor looked up. His expression grew grim as he saw what awaited him. There was a great humming in the room – and the Dome was descending towards them. His hand sought and found Vicki's. He muttered to her out of the corner of his mouth.

'Here, child – take the Web Destructor. We don't want it discovering that – as it did the recorder.'

He nodded ahead and upward at the Dome. Amid the jostling from the Zarbi Vicki took the Destructor and slipped it under her jacket. Angrily Doctor Who attempted to shake off the claws that now gripped him, but the Zarbi thrust him roughly, reeling, towards the spot where the Dome was descending.

The Doctor stood there and it closed about his silvery head. He stood stiffly, hemmed in by Zarbi on all sides, awaiting the verdict of the Voice.

The Zarbi ignored Vicki. She began to edge away towards the *Tardis*' control table.

Now the Voice boomed and surged around the Doctor inside the glassy Dome.

'Your escape attempt failed-ed . . .'

'Escape attempt? My dear whatever-you-are – we went on a little exploration, that's all . . .'

'You lie-ie!' the Voice roared.

'When your creatures found us, we were returning here! Does that sound like an escape to you? Mmm?' Doctor Who retorted.

'The Zarbi you took with you – it is no longer under my control! Why?'

Doctor Who could not repress a chuckle. His face straightened as he realized the gravity of their position and he flung up his head defiantly, bluffing outrageously.

'Oh – so that's my fault too, is it? You know, when your systems break down, you really shouldn't start blaming everybody in sight!'

There was a strange silence. Then the Voice bellowed again, 'I cannot follow your trickery – but that is what it is! You will be brought to the centre! To me!'

Doctor Who stared. He hesitated. A note of uncertainty crept into his voice, but he kept his outward calm.

'And the girl?' he demanded.

'She will be brought with you-ou . . . !'

'If any harm comes to us, I warn you—'.

'Enough . . . !' the Voice roared. 'Your threats are of no interest-st . . . !'

The Dome whisked upward from Doctor Who's head. He turned and saw the Zarbi at the control panel reacting busily to a stream of hummed orders from the flashing panel. The Doctor's guards closed in on him and gripped him. Others turned their attention now to Vicki, hovering at the Doctor's astral table. They pounced on her too, and jostled the two of them towards an opening near the control wall. Vicki fought and kicked, resisting, gasping with fear.

'Doctor – what are they going to do . . . ?'

There was no use keeping the truth from her. Doctor Who said gently, 'Taking us to the centre. Try not to be afraid, my dear . . .'

The Zarbi shoved them roughly through the door.

Barbara and her Menoptera comrades lay scattered behind the scanty cover of the small rocks outside of the Web Headquarters. Barbara turned and raised a beckoning hand towards Hrostar. He came scrambling forward, darting from cover to cover on the way, until he sprawled beside her. He looked over the rock towards the great glowing web.

Barbara whispered to him, 'The Doctor must be in the control room by now.'

Hrostar nodded. 'I'll tell the others.' He darted away again.

Now Barbara signalled to Prapillus, crouched under a near-by rock. The old Menoptera came crawling painfully towards her.

Barbara gestured to where the Zarbi under Prapillus' control hunched motionless on the ground. She pointed towards the web entrance of the great glowing structure.

'Send our Zarbi in – we'll try and follow,' she whispered.

Prapillus nodded. He gestured. The Zarbi rose slowly. It moved like a creature in a dream across the desolate landscape making for the entrance as Prapillus pointed the way commandingly.

The Zarbi nudged and jostled Doctor Who and Vicki deeper down a great glowing tunnel, and, as they lurched and stumbled on, a new noise came to their ears above the humming and chirruping around them.

It was a steady throb-throb, like a gigantic heartbeat. It was so powerful and yet so low-pitched that they felt its beat rather than heard it.

At the end of this corridor a great light pulsed in time with the beat. Doctor Who hesitated as they saw it and nudged Vicki.

'Try and pass me back the Web Destructor now,' he muttered. 'We may not get another chance ...'

He stared ahead and his hand furtively sought Vicki's.

'Come, come – don't worry if these creatures see it now,' he said.

Vicki gulped, 'I ... I haven't got it,' she stammered.

'Of course you have – I gave it to you, remember?'

'I didn't know we'd be leaving the control room. I wanted to ... keep it safe, and ...'

Doctor Who halted and stared. He was jostled on by the Zarbi. He kept looking at Vicki, alarmed now.

'Where is it now?'

'On your control table! I hid it there! Oh – Doctor, I'm *sorry*! I didn't know that—'

Vicki began to sob. Doctor Who masked his grave concern and tried to comfort her. He managed to smile.

'Well, don't distress yourself, child. It's not your fault . . .'

The Zarbi urged the faltering Vicki harshly onward. They moved straight on down the straight long corridor which pulsed so strangely, towards the great throbbing glare of light which grew brighter and brighter at the far end.

Barbara, Hrostar and the others rose silently from their rock cover as they and the Zarbi under Prapillus' control neared the web entrance to the great building.

As their Zarbi halted, a commotion broke out at the entrance.

This time the Zarbi guard challenged it with an excited humming and chirruping.

The controlled Zarbi ignored it. It stepped purposefully on, pausing only to thrust the challenging guard lurching out of the way.

'Now!' Barbara cried. She balanced a stalagmite spear she carried and hurled it.

The spear caught the Zarbi guard and whanged harmlessly away against the creature's hard, shiny shell. But it reared, alarmed, and scampered hastily back into the web entrance.

Hlynia came running to join Barbara as they watched the creature retreat.

'It will bring reinforcements,' Hlynia murmured.

Barbara turned. 'That's what we wanted – isn't it?'

Prapillus now ventured forward and raised his hand towards the web entrance. Inside, they saw the figure of their Zarbi stop, in complete obedience still.

'Into the corridors,' Prapillus cried. 'The Zarbi will find it more difficult to scatter us there!'

He rushed forward. The others followed the valiant old man, hot on his heels. Hrostar gained on Barbara and reached out to stay her.

'Barbara – go back! This is not your war! It is not right that you should risk your life for us!'

Barbara thrust his hand away. 'I'm doing it for my friends as well! Come on!'

She ran swiftly towards the entrance, racing Hrostar and Hilio to be first to the door.

Inside the great web the alarms were sounding.

Barbara leaped through the web entrance and to the astonishment of the younger Menoptera, old Prapillus came panting in right on their heels.

'Hrostar!' he called.

'I'm ready, Prapillus!'

Prapillus pointed ahead. 'Be ready to move up to the next junction of the corridors!' Hrostar nodded and stationed himself ahead of them as Prapillus now gave his attention to controlling their Zarbi captive.

'What are you doing?' Barbara called.

'The Zarbi will have venom-guns,' the old man muttered. 'This is the only way we can stop them. Now – help me with this creature!'

Barbara paused, confused. 'To do what?'

'To *hold* him – you, Hilio and Hlynia. I'm taking off the necklet.'

Prapillus had taken complete charge, and there was no time to argue. Together they held the great Zarbi tight as Prapillus reached up and snatched off the treated slave necklet by which they had controlled it.

Immediately it was free, the Zarbi came to vicious life, striking out and struggling to be free.

Prapillus threw the necklet towards Hrostar who caught it and darted away ahead, running off into a side corridor.

A moment later a knot of Zarbi rounded a bend and rushed into sight, urging a venom-gun forward.

'Look out!' Prapillus called back. 'Sting-gun!'

Barbara, Hilio and Hlynia bore their struggling Zarbi back against the tunnel wall, taking cover behind it. Prapillus backed swiftly to join them, his eye on the evil sting as it leaped forward.

'Hrostar – now!' Prapillus yelled.

As the venom grub came level with the side corridor ahead of them Hrostar leaped out from his hiding-place there, the necklet levelled. The Zarbi saw him and with incredible speed one of them reacted, gestured. The sting slithered to a stop, turned, and pointed its wicked snout. As Hrostar darted towards it, it spat fire.

Hrostar screamed and threw up his hands. He staggered forward, lunged with his last ounce of strength – and clipped the necklet over the snout of the sting creature where it broadened to meet the grub's body.

Then he fell face down on the floor.

The sting creature stopped. Prapillus darted out and gestured. The venom grub wheeled and turned on its masters – the Zarbi. As Prapillus guided it, it levelled its sting straight at them.

The Zarbi reared wildly and scattered back, melting away into side corridors farther up the tunnel, chirruping with panic.

Barbara, Hilio and Hlynia relaxed their combined grip on their captive Zarbi and it, too, scurried away desperately down the main tunnel to join the retreating Zarbi.

Prapillus, pleased, stared down at the motionless sting grub. Hlynia rushed to the fallen Hrostar. She knelt over him and then looked up.

'Hrostar is dead,' she said dully.

At that Hilio moved, snatched up his spar, lashed it savagely across the thick back of the venom grub. The shell cracked. Like a madman, Hilio lashed again. The evil snout snapped. The venom grub rolled over, twitched, and lay still. Only then did Hilio lower his arm. He stared up the corridor, his face dark.

Barbara protested. 'Why destroy it, Hilio? Couldn't we have used it against the Zarbi?'

Prapillus shook his head sadly. He held up the necklet. 'This wouldn't work on a sting creature in that way. It would simply cancel its power. The Zarbi would repel its venom – if they had the sense to realize that. All we can hope to do is to stop *them* from using it, and destroy these evil creatures.'

He pointed at the lifeless sting grub. Hilio reached and snatched up the necklet.

'The next sting is mine!' he snarled.

'It will not be so easy – next time, Hilio,' Prapillus warned him.

Hilio nodded and stared grimly up the corridor.

'Follow,' he barked, and moved along it watchfully. Barbara, Prapillus and Hlynia moved after him. Barbara paused a moment. She looked at the dead Hrostar. His action had saved their lives – for the moment – at the cost of his own.

'Let's hope it was not in vain, Hrostar,' she whispered, and went on up after the others.

Doctor Who and Vicki, surrounded by the jostling escort, had almost reached the end of the huge corridor.

A great webbed gate stretched across it, and through it glared a light of almost hurtful brilliance, pulsing and flashing, at the same time as the low, heavy throbbing almost shook their bodies with its beat.

The Zarbi halted their two captives before the enormous webbed door, and emitted a humming, chirruping call.

Vicki looked up at the door and the searing light beyond and tried to master the sickening fear that welled up within her. She tried bravely to joke.

'We've arrived, Doctor.'

'Yes, my child,' the Doctor answered gravely. 'At least we'll see now what sort of creature this is . . .'

The huge webbed door slid upward and the Zarbi pushed the Doctor and Vicki roughly through it.

They paused on the threshold, blinking painfully as the full blinding power of the great pulsing light from within struck them like a blow. Vicki groped, her eyes narrowed painfully against its brutal glare, as terrified as if it were total darkness.

'Can you see it . . . Doctor . . . can you see . . . ?'

'I . . . can see nothing, child.'

The Zarbi withdrew, closing the immense webbed gate behind them, shutting them in with the great light, the pulsing, the throbbing.

Then the Voice spoke. It boomed almost as hollowly and from as great a depth as it had within the Dome. It grated deeply and echoed all around the chamber.

'Welcome . . . you are the first humans to . . . enter my kingdom-om . . .'

Vicki started to hear the Voice the Doctor had spoken of for the first time. Doctor Who raised a hand and shielded his eyes against the radiance. He spoke in the direction of the sound.

'Who are you? What do you want?'

'Come!' the Voice ordered. 'Approach, earth people! Your cells, your earthly mental processes, will provide my most enriching sustenance yet.'

A realization of what this creature was suddenly dawned on Doctor Who with those words. It was as though all his guessing, his wondering about it had really been a groping search for the right key to the mystery of this Intelligence – and these words had unlocked it in a single sentence.

'You're a parasite!' he exclaimed. 'A super-parasite. Of course!'

'A super-*power*!' the Voice corrected him. 'Absorbing not only territory, but the best of its riches – its energy, culture. The Menoptera are nothing – you and your friends are a choicer prize.'

'What's it *saying*, Doctor?' Vicki whispered above the deep throbbing sound. 'What does it *mean*?'

The Doctor paused.

'It's a kind . . . of spider, Vicki – a cosmic spider!' His face was puckered against the glare. 'It draws its victims in, and when it feasts, it acquires their knowledge . . . their skills . . .'

Vicki started fearfully and turned to look back into the great light, trying to penetrate it. Again the Voice boomed the order.

'Approach . . . approach – you cannot resist my power . . .!'

Vicki suddenly lurched a half-step forward and stood there, wobbling, fighting against a force that drew her inward. Doctor Who flung out a hand, groping in the blazing light to hold her back.

'Don't move, child!' he rapped. 'Stay where you are!'

'I can't help it!' she breathed, half-sobbing with fear. 'Doctor . . . it's . . . pulling me . . .!'

The Voice grated. 'Do not fight against it . . . approach . . . approach . . . both of you . . .!'

'You *mustn't move*, Vicki!' The Doctor called desperately. 'Whatever you do, *don't move*!'

Vicki struggled to remain where she was, but was pulled another inexorable lurching pace forward. Doctor Who, too, felt himself stumbling as he fought to keep his feet planted firmly where they were. The great blurry radiance which fogged the centre of the chamber with its blazing brilliance slowly cleared as they grew accustomed to looking into its glare – and the Doctor saw, for the first time, the outlines, the shape of the thing which controlled this whole planet.

It was this thing which had spawned and propelled the

great web till it reached out across Vortis – this creature alone whose power operated the hordes of Zarbi like an army of puppets. And it was the power of this thing, relayed through its Zarbi slaves, which spat venom through the jets of ordinary living animals and destroyed whatever stood in its way.

The Doctor saw that it was a living thing, all right. It was an enormous oval bladder which seemed composed entirely of light. It stood vertical and revolved on its own axis. As it did so the great light pulsed and throbbed with it. Its blazing elongated shape swelled and shrank in rhythm with the pulses, breathing, like a living lung.

It was towards this weird all-powerful creation, rotating slowly in the centre of the dazzling chamber, that Doctor Who and Vicki were being drawn, fight as they might against it, like tiny pieces of steel towards a colossal magnet.

In the underground caverns beneath the great web, the diggers had struck upward until their spears sank into a soft gluey substance – which, even as they watched, swelled and spat, reaching out and forming new web patterns.

The pigmy-menoptera halted and stared at this substance with slitted eyes. The gluey tentacles glowed and throbbed.

Ian, climbing in their wake, saw the glow pulsing through the darkness and called excitedly to Hetra and Vrestin.

'The web – look! Its roots reach even down into the earth!'

Vrestin climbed upward, finding footholds on the stair-like ledges which the diggers had chopped out as they went.

'It's glowing!' Vrestin panted. 'Throbbing with light pulses!'

'That must mean we're below the centre itself!' Ian exclaimed.

He motioned to the diggers to continue their work. Doubtfully now, afraid, they attacked the earth above them, then paused. The reaching masses of the web grew brighter as they inched upward. 'That's it!' Ian urged them. 'Dig towards the light!' Follow the brightest strands! They will take us into its heart!'

This news halted the diggers. They wavered and paused

doubtfully. But they gathered their resolve and resumed their attack on the roof, taking courage from Ian's confidence. The heavy measured throbbing from above was now pulsing loudly in their ears.

Barbara, Prapillus, Hilio and the girl Menoptera Hlynia turned into a new, larger corridor and came stealthily down it towards the sound of a distant chirruping.

Barbara peered forward and could make out the details of a control panel at the far end of this corridor. Silently she motioned her companions on towards it. They crept along, staring cautiously all around them.

They had nearly reached the entrance to the chamber at the end of the corridor when Barbara halted them with a sign. She ventured forward to the threshold, and flattening herself against the corridor wall, peered inward.

Hastily she ducked back and crouched with the others.

'Zarbi!' she said.

Hilio came darting from the rear to join Barbara.

'How many?'

'I only saw one,' Barbara answered, keeping her eyes on the door.

'With venom-guns?'

Barbara shook her head. 'No – alone, I . . . think . . .'

Hilio darted on to the door, gripping the necklet he carried, and peered inward too. Prapillus tiptoed up to join him. He touched Hilio's winged shoulder.

'Make sure you stop it reaching the control panel, Hilio!' he urged.

Hilio nodded curtly. He tensed himself – and then charged through the doorway and into the chamber.

The lone Zarbi on duty turned and saw Hilio hurl himself forward, the necklet levelled at the creature's throat. The Zarbi in alarm chirruped, dodged, and lashed swiftly with a steely claw, knocking Hilio sideways in his rush. It turned and scampered across towards the control panel. Hilio, recovering, lunged between the creature and the glowing web map, paused, feinted, then charged. He gripped the Zarbi's foreclaw, wrenched it aside, thrust at its throat – and clipped home the sense-deadening necklet.

Immediately the Zarbi stiffened, and calmed.

Barbara, Prapillus and Hlynia hurried now through the doorway towards Hilio. Prapillus nodded with delighted approval at the immobilized Zarbi.

'Well done, Hilio!' he beamed.

Hilio reached out a hand and took the stalagmite spar which Hlynia was carrying. He whirled it and smashed it across the control panel, again and again.

Vicki and Doctor Who now stood perilously near the great revolving ellipse which puffed in and out and pulsed with dazzling light. They were straining desperately backward, but the pull which drew them in towards the blinding centre grew irresistibly stronger.

The whole floor beneath their lurching feet was a gigantic, pulsating web, its mesh glittering as the super-parasite, the creature Doctor Who had called a cosmic spider, rotated and breathed.

Vicki was exhausted, and with the tiredness her will was fading.

'I can't struggle ... any more ... Doctor!' she moaned. 'I *can't* ...!'

Doctor Who looked desperately all around them. They were shut in alone with this burning eye-shaped monster, and all help against its immense power seemed far away.

But he urged Vicki still. 'Don't give in now, child. We *must* not let it win!'

'But, Doctor ... there's no chance ... nobody to help us now! And it was my fault ... my fault.'

She sobbed as she felt the deadly force pulling her trembling legs forward. The Voice boomed closer now, on a great note of triumph.

'Approach ... approach ... what I will assimilate from you will enable me to reach beyond this galaxy, into the solar system ... to pluck from the earth its myriad techniques ... in its hundredth Christian millennium ...!'

The Doctor muttered as, in spite of himself, he lurched forward a step ... then another ...

Suddenly a new note overlaid the echoes of the booming Voice. Doctor Who stiffened and strained his ears to catch it.

Yes – a humming, a throbbing of the same sort as they had heard from the communicators on the panel in the control room. It was speckled with an alarmed chirruping.

The noise faded again.

Then the Voice boomed out harshly, close.

'Section Q not responding to command? Aliens in control!'

A roar of rage accompanied this surprise and Doctor Who lifted his head. He turned to Vicki and flashed her a triumphant look.

'That sounds like help, child. Don't give up ... don't give up ...!'

But still they felt the pull of the cosmic spider drawing them in towards it, and lurched another agonizing step or two, fighting against it.

Barbara and the Menoptera stared around the control room.

'The Doctor and Vicki should have got to the centre by now,' Barbara murmured to Hlynia.

'Yes ... we must trust in their success.'

Prapillus had wandered inquisitively over towards the astral map. He called, 'Barbara ...!'

Barbara moved to join the old Menoptera. His eyes on the controls of Doctor Who's control table were alive with interest. He pointed at the communicator knobs.

'Does this thing work?'

Barbara hesitated. 'Well, yes – I think so.'

'Could we contact our invasion forces on it?' Prapillus demanded. 'Warn our people ...?'

Barbara shrugged doubtfully. 'Well ... yes – if I can find the frequency. I've only ever seen the Doctor use it once.'

She reached and adjusted the knobs, pointing to the transmission and wavelength controls. 'Now ... that ... and there ... you can try it now – this is the speaker.'

Prapillus bent towards the speaker. He switched on the speaker button and called in his high-pitched treble. 'Vortis to main force. Vortis to main force ... warning. Repeat – warning ... Electron-guns are useless against the Zarbi ... Sayo Plateau heavily ambushed ... await instructions ... acknowledge please ... over.'

He paused, switching over to 'receive' at Barbara's silent direction, and listened.

They waited but no answering sound came – not even the whispering spatial echoes that told of a transmitter switched on and operating on the Menoptera's wavelength.

'Either they haven't heard us,' Hilio said. 'Or, they don't trust us.'

'*Or* I haven't set it right,' Barbara said, staring at the set and frowning. She took over and checked the controls. She cleared the table of its clutter and as she did so an implement caught her eye. She held it up. It was the Web Destructor, the precious weapon they had entrusted to Doctor Who! She wheeled.

'Prapillus – look!'

Prapillus and the others stared in dismay.

'We must take it to the centre ourselves!' Hilio snapped.

'But ... the doctor – what happened?' Barbara stammered. 'Why didn't *he* take it?'

'They must have discovered his plan,' Prapillus answered sombrely.

Hlynia said. 'It was hidden under that equipment, why?'

'We haven't the time to stand guessing!' Barbara said. She turned towards the big doorway which opened off the control room into the largest corridor, 'Let's hurry! Please ...!'

Barbara strode to the door. Hilio took up the Web Destructor and hastened to catch her up. Prapillus and Hlynia followed, quickening their pace.

They came stealthily into the vast corridor and moved down it. From the far end a glow shone so brightly that at first Barbara thought it was a furnace. She saw that it came from beyond a huge webbed door.

She and her companions pressed on stealthily. They paused as they heard a chirruping sound somewhere and darted into a recess – a short side corridor. Hilio peered out while they waited. The corridor remained empty.

'All clear,' Hilio reported, and they emerged into the main corridor again and headed down towards the huge door.

'Can you hear it?' Hlynia whispered suddenly. She pressed her delicate hands to her temples.

'Hear what?' Barbara asked.

'A . . . sort of . . . throbbing! Oh, it makes my head spin!' Hlynia exclaimed.

Hilio came abreast of Barbara and tapped the Web Destructer he carried. 'Remember – whatever this creature proves to be, this must be aimed towards its darker side, where it will be more vulnerable.'

Barbara nodded.

'. . . and,' Hilio reminded her, 'we must all try and capture its attention. The one best placed will fire this and detonate the cell mutator. Understood?'

'Understood,' Barbara answered.

'Zarbi!' Prapillus suddenly yelled.

Barbara, Hilio and Hlynia froze in their steps. From a recess ahead of them a squad of Zarbi had scurried into view, driving before them the squat hulk of a sting grub, which wheeled and headed down towards them. Barbara and the Menoptera looked wildly about for cover.

'There's no going back!' Prapillus shouted. We must rush them! It needs only one of us to get through with the Destructor! Come on!'

And the old Menoptera led them impetuously, charging down the corridor to meet the advancing Zarbi and their venom grub. With only a moment's hesitation, the others leaped forward to join Prapillus in his charge.

The leading Zarbi halted, and its foreclaw swivelled till the sting's snout levelled at Prapillus and the others running and dodging towards them.

Suddenly all the Zarbi, including their leader froze. The creatures stood like graven images as the charge carried

Barbara, Prapillus and the other two Menoptera clean through their ranks. Barbara paused for a moment of wild disbelief as she looked back and saw the Zarbi still halted where they were.

'They let us through!' she shouted unbelievingly. 'They didn't do a thing to stop us! Why?'

Prapillus paused, looked back, and then ahead – ominously.

'We were expected,' he muttered. He braced his shoulders. 'Well – let us not disappoint ... whatever awaits us.'

He pointed at the door before them with the fierce glow of light beyond it, and took the lead again, marching grimly towards it.

'It may be expecting us – but I doubt if it will be expecting *this*,' Hilio said, and tapped the Web Destructor he carried.

As they reached the vast web doors they paused a moment, wondering how to force them. Hlynia looked back. She nudged Barbara and pointed.

Behind them the Zarbi had turned and had moved silently after them, not attempting to molest them – merely shadowing their progress. The Zarbi halted now and watched from a distance.

Hlynia was uneasy. 'Whatever is in there thinks itself strong enough without *them*,' she murmured.

Then the big web doors swung back silently inward and the intense light beyond it bathed them all in its glare. Barbara and the Menoptera moved warily in, Hilio with the Web Destructor at the ready.

They halted and blinked and could see nothing in the blinding glare which now enveloped them. No sooner had they entered than they suddenly felt the pull of an immense, unseen power. The force of it made them lurch forward clumsily, clouding their thinking, their resolve, so that they had stumbled several paces before Barbara shouted.

'Stop! Wait! Don't go any farther!'

But the powerful force field in this dazzling chamber seemed to have affected the Menoptera more than Barbara. They did not appear to have heard her. The three of them –

even the valiant Prapillus – were shuffling, blank-eyed towards a fierce, blinding core of light which pulsed and glared in the centre of the chamber.

'Hilio!' Barbara shouted. 'The Destructor . . .!'

Hilio turned and stared dazedly back at her – but made no other move. It was as though he no longer had a will of his own. Barbara darted forward and snatched the Web Destructor from the Menoptera's nerveless hands. She wheeled and pointed it towards the source of all this light – the great, revolving bladder-shaped organ which breathed, whose brilliant glare stung her eyes and dazzled her.

Several paces in front of Barbara, and now perilously near to the blazing centre, Vicki – dazed, sleepy as though drugged, but still resisting – heard Barbara's voice. She turned.

'Barbara?' she called weakly. 'Barbara . . .?'

Dimly, as she narrowed her eyes, Barbara made out the silhouette of Vicki ahead of her, haloed against the great light . . . then the frock-coated figure of the Doctor, oddly pathetic and helpless as the old man stood and fought against the power that drew him into its vortex. The silvery head turned. Hazily the Doctor saw Barbara.

He called hoarsely, 'Use the Destructor . . . use . . . the . . . Destructor . . .!'

Barbara lurched forward, pulled violently, and brought up the Web Destructor, peering to find the centre of the target in the blazing fog of light.

'The dark side . . .' she muttered despairingly. 'Hilio said . . . I must aim at . . . the dark side . . .!'

She summoned her strength and darted across to one side, her steps stumbling and sluggish against the immense pull inward. She wheeled, shading her view, her hand trembling on the lever of the Destructor.

'There is . . . *no dark side* . . .!'

Then she heard the Voice boom out. '. . . your struggles . . . are futile-ile . . . Approach . . . earth people . . . approach . . .!'

169

Barbara saw the helpless figures of the Doctor and Vicki as they moved inward, their legs braced and struggling as if caught in a mighty undertow.

Barbara fought a further step sideways to keep the Doctor out of her line of fire. Desperately now, she levelled and aimed the Destructor at the fiery mass whirling on its pivot in the centre of the chamber.

Nothing happened.

'It's ... not working ...!' she gasped, and pressed the trigger again.

She stepped forward. Perhaps if she got in closer ...

But as she did so the field of force closed around her and the pull on her grew immensely more powerful.

She staggered forward, stared about, and saw a fissure suddenly open up in the floor beneath the great sparkling web. A strange, curly spear poked through it, then hands gripped the floor and the figure of a man heaved his body up through the crack and stood gazing blindly about him on the vast floor of the chamber.

It was Ian!

'Ian . . .!' screamed Barbara.

Ian turned to look towards the voice and then threw up his arms against the light which blotted out all else. He staggered and fell, groping blindly around him, lost. Barbara saw that they could all now count their life in seconds – and that everything now depended on her.

She was dragged a step closer to the flashing light and raised the Destructor. She fired it again, this time holding her hand clamped down on its electronic lever.

The Voice droned on echoingly, apparently unharmed, addressing them all.

'You have not . . . the power . . . power . . . I . . . Master . . . of . . . you . . .'

Barbara kept the Destructor pointed at the heart of the monstrous shape and breathed a prayer, blinking against the light, steadying her hand to keep the Destructor on its target.

Was it because she was dazzled – or was this monstrous creature changing its shape? Was she imagining it – that its breathing was growing ragged, its steady pulsing light changing into an irregular, staccato pattern, first bright, then darkening to a dull glow . . .?

The Voice became more bronchial, more hesitant, and stumbled.

'. . . Master . . . the . . . the . . .'

She was *not* dreaming! She held the trigger lever of the Destructor grimly pressed, its squat muzzle pointing unwaveringly towards the searingly bright Ellipse, and the Voice rose to a whining scream.

'. . . the . . . the . . . Universe . . .'

Suddenly the Voice choked, and was silent. Its bronchial wheezing faded, gasping, and was stilled. The pulsating light within the bladder dwindled slowly down to a ruddy glow – and then blanked out. A darkness came into the room, and with it, a coldness.

The lifeless bladder shape continued to revolve, slackly, without breath, slowing, and spun tiredly to a stop.

The silence in the room now was total.

The centre of all this evil which had seized Vortis in its grip shuddered once, and was still.

Barbara dropped the Destructor. It clattered through the now-lifeless web on to the floor below.

Doctor Who roused himself and stepped towards what was left of the Intelligence. Vicki joined him. Ian had picked up the Destructor and weighing it curiously in his hand, stared around the room.

'It's dead,' Vicki said in a flat, tired voice, 'dead . . .'

Ian nodded and put his arm around her. He turned her head away from it.

'It's all over,' he said gently. 'We can leave now.'

Doctor Who's control table with its astral map and its clutter of equipment had been loaded back into *Tardis*.

The Doctor stood with Prapillus before the smashed remains of the Zarbi's control panel. He eyed the Web Destructor admiringly and laid it down.

'A giant can die, from the sting of a fly,' he quoted. 'Yes . . . an interesting weapon.'

'If I had not lived to see this – I would have counted my life entirely wasted,' old Prapillus said. His voice trembled.

Doctor Who put a hand on the old man's shoulder. He said, 'It was your wisdom, Prapillus, that helped us to defeat this creature – and all it controlled.'

He turned towards the ship. Barbara and Vicki were near the door, waiting. The Doctor paused and said to the old Menoptera, 'Well – there's nothing more to keep us here. It's . . . time to leave.'

He held out his hand to Prapillus, and smiled. 'Goodbye.'

Prapillus clung to the Doctor's hand. 'You must stay!' he

insisted. 'All of you! Share in the adventure of a new civilization! We need you!'

Doctor Who shook his head.

'No – you don't need us. You are more than a man of science, Prapillus. Yours is the wisdom of a ruler.'

The Doctor strode to the ship. Barbara was waving to the Menoptera grouped in the control room – to Hlynia, Hilio and Prapillus.

'Good-bye!' she called. 'And . . . thank you.'

She climbed inside. Vicki followed her.

Ian shook Vrestin's hand. Vrestin looked at him and said, 'You will come back?'

Ian shrugged. 'Perhaps,' he smiled.

'Come on now, Chesterton,' the Doctor said. He halted and surveyed Ian, who was rather dishevelled from his adventures underground, his usually immaculate suit stained and crumpled.

'Hmmph!' the Doctor grunted. 'I suppose the least I can do is find you somewhere where they have neckties.'

'That's right,' Ian reminded him, following the Doctor inside. 'With green and black stripes, for dear old Coal Hill School . . .'

'Huh!' the Doctor snorted, 'I didn't know they had colours in a kindergarten!'

He turned into the ship.

The doors closed. A whirring started up – the smooth steady noises of *Tardis*' machinery, no longer hampered by the force that had drawn it on to Vortis.

As the Menoptera stood and watched, the police-box outlines of *Tardis* melted and faded gently until the contours of the control room showed clear through it.

Then it was gone.

The silence among the Menoptera was broken by the lovely Hlynia. 'It . . . disappeared . . .!' she breathed.

Prapillus nodded. 'Their deeds have written the greatest page in our history,' he murmured. Then he became brisk. He turned to the others.

'We must welcome the invasion forces. Come!'

The old Menoptera stumped off, leading the way, and paused as the hand of the aged leader of the pigmy-menoptera, Hetra, reached out to stay him.

'And – my people . . .?' Hetra quavered.

Prapillus smiled down at him and his dwarfish squad of comrades.

'They will take their rightful place – join us in rebuilding Vortis.' He put his arm on Hetra's shoulder.

'And the Zarbi?' It was Hilio who spoke. He pointed to a cluster of Zarbi crouched mutely in a corner of the control room – aimless, leaderless, waiting docilely now for someone to command them.

'They too have a place in the order of things here,' Prapillus said. He led his small group towards an opening in the control room wall. Here the webbing had already melted and sagged away, and through the gaps in the crumbling remains of the great web they could see the landscape of Vortis.

The old man stood there for a moment, looking out upon his planet.

It seemed to be growing lighter. A radiance shone from behind the crags, gilding their outlines and dispelling their shadows, like the rising of a sun.

'DOCTOR WHO'

TERRANCE DICKS
Doctor Who and The
0426200373 **Android Invasion** **90p**

Doctor Who and the
0426201086 **Androids of Tara** **75p**

Doctor Who and The
0426201043 **Armageddon Factor** **85p**

IAN MARTER
Doctor Who and The Ark
0426116313 **in Space** **90p**

Doctor Who and The
0426116747 **Brain of Morbius** **95p**

TERRANCE DICKS
Doctor Who and The
0426117034 **Claws of Axos** **75p**

DAVID FISHER
Doctor Who and The
042620123X **Creature from the Pit** **90p**

BRIAN HAYLES
Doctor Who and The Curse
0426114981 **of Peladon** **75p**

GERRY DAVIS
0426114639 **Doctor Who and The Cybermen** **85p**

BARRY LETTS
0426113322 **Doctor Who and The Daemons** **£1.50**

DAVID WHITAKER
0426101103 **Doctor Who and The Daleks** **85p**

TERRANCE DICKS
Doctor Who and The Dalek
042611244X **Invasion of Earth** **£1.25**

Doctor Who and The Day
0426103807 **of the Daleks** **85p**

Prices are subject to alteration

STAR Books are obtainable from many booksellers and newsagents. If you have any difficulty please send purchase price plus postage on the scale below to:

Star Cash Sales
P.O. Box 11
Falmouth
Cornwall
OR
Star Book Service,
G.P.O. Box 29,
Douglas,
Isle of Man,
British Isles.

While every effort is made to keep prices low, it is sometimes necessary to increase prices at short notice. Star Books reserve the right to show new retail prices on covers which may differ from those advertised in the text or elsewhere.

Postage and Packing Rate
UK: 40p for the first book, 18p for the second book and 13p for each additional book ordered to a maximum charge of £1·49p. BFPO and EIRE: 40p for the first book, 18p for the second book, 13p per copy for the next 7 books, thereafter 7p per book. Overseas: 60p for the first book and 18p per copy for each additional book.